**'You're a dan...
know, Cara Ga...**

She stared at him, ...
echoed. 'Me?'

Finn nodded. 'Yes, you. I don't know you, and I don't know how serious you are about getting away… Have you any idea of what you want to do now? A plan, maybe?'

'A plan?' she echoed blankly. She had never in her life before been asked such a question. Everybody else always made plans for her. Suddenly Cara found herself thinking of possibilities and consequences. And all of them looked black.

She eyed the stranger a little doubtfully. 'What about you? Do you have a plan?'

He scratched his jaw. 'Oh, plenty,' he agreed. 'But unfortunately I made most of them before I attended your wedding. And none of them included a runaway bride with half the thugs in Naples on her tail.'

Sally Carr trained as a journalist and has worked on several national newspapers. She was brought up in the West Indies and her travels have taken her nearly all over the world, including Tibet, Russia and North America. She lives with her husband, two dogs, three goldfish and six hens in an old hunting lodge in Northamptonshire, and has become an expert painter and decorator. She enjoys walking, gardening, and playing the clarinet.

Recent titles by the same author:

HONEYMOON ASSIGNMENT

STOLEN BRIDE

BY
SALLY CARR

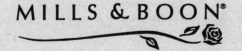

MILLS & BOON®

All the characters in this book have no existence outside the imagination of the author, and have no relation whatsoever to anyone bearing the same name or names. They are not even distantly inspired by any individual known or unknown to the author, and all the incidents are pure invention.

*First published in Great Britain 1997
Harlequin Mills & Boon Limited,
Eton House, 18-24 Paradise Road, Richmond, Surrey TW9 1SR*

© Sally Carr 1997

ISBN 0 263 80157 8

*Set in Times Roman 10 on 12 pt.
02-9706-55271 C1*

*Printed and bound in Great Britain
by Mackays of Chatham PLC, Chatham*

CHAPTER ONE

IT WAS cold in the church, away from the pounding heat outside, but Cara felt a chill that had nothing to do with the temperature.

She took a glance once more at the man standing next to her, and then down at her dress, the heavy silk dragging away from her waist like an ice slope. In a few moments she was going to marry a man she knew she couldn't love, and there was nothing she could do about it. She couldn't back down now.

Behind her, she knew, the church was packed with the two families who looked upon this moment as the final seal on the relationship between them. A medieval view, maybe, but one that still held in this part of Italy. Especially when it concerned the future good fortune of the family.

Cara clasped and unclasped her fingers. What was it the priest had just said? By her side, Luca seemed to be taking everything in, listening gravely to the man's words. His neck, reddened where he had shaved it, bulged slightly over his collar. It reminded her suddenly of a wild turkey her uncle had once shot, and she looked hurriedly away.

There were huge candles, as thick as her arm, burning everywhere in the church, their flames steady in the still air. And there was incense, too, its sharp smell pricking her nostrils. She shook her head irritably. Why did this ceremony keep reminding her of a funeral? It was supposed to be the happiest day of her life.

5

She shot another surreptitious glance at her bride-groom. She had always known Luca. Treated him as the big brother she had never had. And when he had sug-gested marriage she had been initially excited by the idea. She had never been encouraged to have a career, and being the wife of an important man like Luca seemed rather glamorous. She had been very flattered that he had chosen her.

How foolish she had been. She stared woodenly at the priest and bit her lip. It hadn't taken her that long to realise that Luca had chosen her because... well, be-cause it made good business sense. Her uncle was one of the most powerful men in this part of Italy, and whoever married her could soon follow suit.

But her dawning realisation over the past few weeks that Luca didn't love her hadn't actually hurt as much as she thought it would. Why *was* that? And then there was the discovery last night that he had a mistress, too. In fact, if she wasn't mistaken, the woman was at the back of the church right at this minute. She quelled the urge to turn and stare at her.

Everything was going so smoothly. So fast. She shivered again and then stiffened as the priest turned to her. All she had to do was agree with him. She stared at Luca and swallowed as her eyes met his. If anything, she was slightly taller than him, and he had used that often to make her feel clumsy and awkward. The priest repeated the question, and still she could say nothing.

Behind her she could feel the congregation stirring. It was right that she should hesitate, they seemed to be saying, but not this much. Just who did she think she was?

Cara half turned to Uncle Pancrazio for support, but he merely smiled and motioned her to carry on. She jerked her head round and looked at Luca once more. His hard brown slightly bloodshot eyes stared coldly into hers, and suddenly her mind was made up. She shook her head. 'No,' she whispered at last.

Had anybody heard? Or had she merely thought she had spoken? She scrunched up a handful of white silk in her left hand and gripping it tightly, she repeated the word more loudly. 'No.'

There was a stunned silence in the church, and she swallowed hard at the expression on Luca's face. 'I can't marry you.' She forced the words out. 'Truly. I thought I could love you, but I can't. Please don't be upset. You ought to find—'

But there was an uproar in the church by now, and Luca was turning to the priest. 'Get on with the ceremony,' he ordered.

The priest looked worriedly at Cara and then at the rest of the congregation. There were too many men in rather bulky jackets for him to refuse.

Half-unbelieving that she was being ignored, Cara turned to her relatives. 'Uncle Pancrazio,' she pleaded, 'you've got to stop this. I don't love Luca. I can't go through with it.'

He looked at her for a long moment, but when he replied it was to Luca, not her. 'It's just nerves,' he replied at last, and then signalled to the priest. 'Carry on. There is no problem.'

Cara stared at him dumbly as Luca's fingers enclosed her wrist and pulled her to his side. 'You will pay for shaming me like this,' he grated. 'I—'

'Just stop right there,' said a new voice. Cara turned wildly, her wrist burning in Luca's grip, to see the whole congregation staring at a lone man standing in the aisle. He was tall, taller than Luca, with dark hair and deep blue eyes. Everyone, including the many bodyguards lining the pews, seemed mesmerised by him.

Luca spun round and Cara, stumbling a little, was forced against him. Carefully she righted herself, holding herself as far away from him as she could.

But Luca tightened his grip, and she gasped as his fingers bit into her flesh. 'Who are you to stop this wedding?' he roared. 'What right do you have here?'

His voice boomed around the church, echoed and died away. Only silence was left. So sudden and so deep it seemed a physical thing. All her relatives, everyone she knew, Luca's family, her uncle's business colleagues, people who together could make more noise than an average football crowd just by saying their prayers, seemed struck dumb. Even Luca seemed suddenly uncertain, his authority reduced to blustering.

Cara's eyes rose to meet the stranger's, and she felt an odd little lift in her heart. 'I have the oldest right in the world,' he drawled. 'This woman just happens to be my wife.'

Her breath seemed to catch in her throat at his words. She could feel Luca staring at her, questioning the stranger's words, but she wouldn't return the look, knowing even he could read the truth in her eyes.

He was coming closer now, the stranger, that long-legged stride looking so slow and in reality so fast. He was wearing a blue linen shirt and white chinos, his hair not black as she had thought, but a deep dark brown, his eyes as blue as a summer sky at midnight.

He had a look in those eyes that dared her to tell the truth, and trusted her not to. The look in the eyes of a man determined to release a wild thing from a trap, even though it might turn on him.

He strolled up to her, and seemingly with no effort at all, took her hand from Luca's. She did not resist, even though she could feel the eyes of every single one of her relatives staring at her in pure shock. And still they were silent.

She knew how they felt. It was as though she was being hypnotised. As though she was dreaming. Her fingers felt cold in his warm ones, and she realised suddenly she was shivering uncontrollably.

He nodded curtly at Luca and then looked at her once more. 'Come along, darling.'

She looked at her fingers almost with surprise as they curled instinctively in his, and then, as she gazed into his eyes once more, she gave him the ghost of a smile and let him lead her towards the door.

'It is a lie!' shouted Uncle Pancrazio, his voice echoing around the church's high ceiling. 'What do you think you are doing! Of course she is not married.'

Cara looked into the stranger's eyes and then at her uncle. 'It is true.' She forced the words out, feeling oddly light-headed at the lie she was telling. Was it really her speaking? 'Last summer—'

'Just keep walking,' whispered the stranger, urging her along as she gabbled at her uncle. 'Whatever happens, don't stop.'

'Last summer!' roared her uncle. 'You faithless— I will kill you both!'

'Run!' yelled the stranger, pulling her out of the church and down the sweeping stone steps. 'There's a killer in there!' he shouted at a knot of bodyguards, now bounding towards them from the waiting cars, already loosening their jackets and reaching inside for their guns. 'Quick! I'll look after her.'

As the chaos of shouting, milling bodies erupted in the church doorway, Cara breathlessly stumbled almost headlong down the steps and then down the deserted street. The stranger was fumbling in his pockets as he ran, pulling out some keys and then opening a car door. He got in and pushed open the door on the other side. 'Get in,' he ordered.

Cara stood irresolute. 'But—' she began.

'No buts,' he snapped. 'We haven't time. Your family will come round that corner in ten seconds flat, and they're not going to be carrying violin cases.'

Cara took one wild glance back and then somehow squeezed herself and the billowing dress into the passenger seat. Her veil parted from the wreath of fresh flowers on her head and bobbed briefly in the air behind them before dragging down onto the dust. It was the last thing she saw before the stranger wrenched the car round a tight bend and she finally managed to shut the door.

They drove in silence for several miles, the stranger concentrating tautly on driving as fast as he could, his eyes constantly flicking to the rear-view mirror.

Cara tightly clasped her hands, which were trembling almost uncontrollably. Was this really happening? It was so... She shrugged and gave up looking for a description. Her brain seemed to have simply frozen in shock.

She pinched the skin on the back of her hand. Could she be dreaming all this? It was hot in the car, and the sun was blazing straight in her eyes. Blinking a little, she moved her legs slightly, and the silk of her dress rustled coldly against her skin. She definitely wasn't dreaming.

She looked at the stranger out of the corner of her eye. What on earth had she done? He could be anybody. He could be the sort of attacker her uncle and Luca were always on guard against. And she had actually let him take her away. Luca had once called her stupid, she remembered, and she had been furiously angry. Maybe he had been right after all.

She turned her head to look carefully at the stranger's face and then back at her lap. 'Who are you?' she said at last. And then without waiting for an answer demanded, 'Why are you doing this? Where are you taking me? Are you kidnapping me? What—'

He lifted one hand off the steering wheel, and she instinctively recoiled. Was he going to hit her, like Luca had once done? But the stranger was merely holding his hand, palm outward, like a traffic policeman.

"My name is Finn Cormac,' he said at last.

English. He was speaking English. But how did he know she would understand? Her eyes widened at the implications of that. No one had spoken English to her for a long, long time. But it was not something she could ever forget how to speak. It was the language of her childhood, of happy times, of the finishing school she had been to when she was eighteen, when she had had her one and only glimpse of freedom.

She stared at him, wondering exactly how much he did know about her. 'But who—' she began.

'No.' He waggled his hand and she fell silent. 'If you're going to jabber at me, you can get out of the car. Now is not the time for twenty questions.'

Her mouth closed and she looked at him warily. He didn't look like a kidnapper. But then what did one look like? And besides, it had been her defiance at the altar that had set this whole thing in motion.

She subsided in her seat, confused by the strangeness of his name and the unreality of what was going on. Questions still buzzed around her brain, but she recognised the sense of what he had said. Now was not the time for them.

'I am Carenza Gambini,' she said at last. 'But everyone calls me Cara.'

He nodded. 'I know.'

She breathed in deeply, then looked sidewise at him. He was driving very fast, with utter concentration on the road ahead. She almost didn't like to disturb him. She tried to think of what her family was doing. Her uncle had been furious. The way he had shouted at her had been almost enough to stop her in her tracks.

And he had turned so paper white when she had followed the stranger that he had looked ill. She felt a sudden shaft of guilt and then thought about the way Luca had pulled her to him. Did *he* care enough about her to follow?

'Do you think Luca will really come after me?' she asked tentatively.

'Are you joking?' demanded Finn, his foot hard on the accelerator. 'Is this Italy or Iceland?'

She breathed out slowly. Of course Luca would come after her. They all would. It had been a stupid question. She knew her family better than anyone. But she had been thinking in terms of how Luca felt about her. Maybe he did love her, after all. Maybe she had just made a terrible mistake.

'He doesn't love me,' she offered, hoping Finn would contradict her. Hoping she had been wrong.

'You're his property, sweetheart,' replied Finn matter-of-factly. 'And you've hurt his pride.'

She felt as though all the air had been knocked out of her. She had just heard, for the first time, someone else—and a complete stranger, at that—express all her secret doubts about the way Luca regarded her—that she was a piece of property. Valuable, maybe, in terms of what marrying her meant. But that was all.

It was something that up until now she thought only she knew. Just who was this man sitting next to her? Helping to boot Luca so surely, right in the middle of his pride?

'Maybe he won't...hurt you,' she offered, not sure at all what she was saying. 'I mean, when I've explained...'

'I heard you trying a bit of explaining at the altar,' replied Finn drily. 'Maybe I'm not very observant, but somehow, he didn't look too bowled over by your reasoning.'

'He's...he's very hot-blooded,' began Cara.

'So am I,' drawled Finn, taking the turn for the *autostrada*. 'And I'd like to stay that way.'

The entrance to the *autostrada* was getting closer, but before they reached it, Finn took a sharp right turn down a cart track into a small wood. He drove carefully through the trees, the car's suspension protesting loudly at the pits and bumps, before coming to a stop as the trees began to thin out by the side of another road.

He switched off the ignition and looked at her thoughtfully. 'Okay,' he said at last. 'We'll wait here until dark. I don't want to take any chances of someone spotting you. I don't think anyone saw the car, and only an idiot would expect us to hide right under your relatives' noses.' He shrugged. 'Not that Luca is exactly in the genius class. But I reckon this is our best chance. We'll be all right here for a while.'

She breathed out, a little shakily, noting the use of the word *we* and not sure what it implied. 'Thanks,' she said. 'But I want to know—'

He sighed and she stopped, uncertain once more about the kind of man she was dealing with. 'Don't thank me,' he drawled. 'You're in deep trouble, if you hadn't already realised it.' He waved his hand at the trees and smiled. 'We are not out of the woods yet.'

She shook her head. 'I don't care,' she said in a low voice. 'Nothing could be worse than being Luca's wife.'

Finn shifted easily in his seat. 'Well, there's something in that,' he conceded.

She decided to begin again. 'Who are you? Are you...' She swallowed. 'Are you someone with a grudge against my uncle?'

He looked at her reflectively. 'No,' he said at last. 'And before you start on that catalogue of questions you've obviously got, I might as well say that I'm not sure I want to tell you too much about me. You're a rather dangerous woman to know, Cara Gambini.'

She stared at him, amazed. 'Dangerous?' she echoed. 'Me?'

He nodded. 'Yes, you. I don't know you, and I don't know how serious you are about getting away from your family.'

'I want to get away from Luca, not my family,' she said hotly.

'Is there a difference?' he asked gently.

There was silence while Cara looked woodenly at her dress. Then he asked, 'Have you any idea what you want to do now? A plan, maybe?'

'A plan?' she echoed blankly. She had never in her life been asked such a question. Everybody else always made plans for her. Suddenly Cara found herself thinking of possibilities and consequences. And all of them looked black.

She eyed the stranger doubtfully. 'What about you? Do you have a plan?'

He scratched his jaw. 'Oh, plenty,' he agreed. 'But unfortunately I made most of them before I attended your wedding. And none of them included a runaway bride with half the thugs in Naples on her tail.'

She bit her lip and stared at him in astonishment. 'You mean you have no idea what we're going to do at all?'

He gazed levelly at her. 'No.'

She met his eyes and noticed little dark flecks in the deep blue. With an impatient shake of her head, she tore her gaze away and stared out the window. For the first time in her life, she was truly on her own. And she would have to start making some decisions. Fast.

'Okay,' she said at last, a lump rising in her throat as she grasped the door handle. 'I'll get out of your way then.'

He reached across her, his hand on hers, her body stilling at the close contact. His face was only inches from her own, his eyes probing deep into hers. Then he pulled back, her hand imprisoned in his, and gazed at her for a few moments.

'Let's start again, shall we?' he said softly. 'First of all, is there any place that you could safely go? Somewhere Luca and your uncle won't be able to coerce you?'

'There is only my uncle's home,' she said in a low voice. Finn was stroking the back of her fingers with his thumb, almost as if it was helping him think. Her first instinct, to pull away completely, slowly melted at the oddly comforting sensation.

'Maybe,' she began diffidently, 'maybe it would be all right if I went home. If I tell them it wasn't nerves, that I truly don't love Luca, then maybe they'll listen.'

'Really?' Finn drawled. His eyes gazed into hers, and she reddened and looked away.

'I'm sure my uncle wants only what is best for me,' she said in low voice.

'Uh-huh,' he replied, his tone loaded with disbelief, and she glanced angrily at him.

'Who are you to pass such judgement on my family?' she demanded.

'Let's say I'm an interested observer,' he said at last.

'Observer?' she echoed. 'What did you say your name was?'

'Finn—'

'Cormac!' she interjected, pulling her hand away and glaring at him. 'Finn Cormac. I know now! You are the...' She tried to think of a suitable swear word and failed. 'The...thing who wrote all those lies about Luca's family. You made millions out of blackening his name. You—'

He held up his hand. 'Save it,' he interrupted. 'In the first place, everything I wrote was true. Luca is just one step ahead of the police at the moment, and two steps from a very long jail term. And in the second, the money I made out of that book, I earned. Unlike the fortune his family has extorted and stolen and been bribed with over the last thirty years.'

Her jaw dropped. 'That's a lie,' she whispered.

'Okay.' He shrugged. 'It's a lie, and your jilted bride-groom is a saint in disguise. So what are you going to do about it?'

She jerked open the car door. 'I'm going home,' she snarled, angry tears beginning to fill her eyes.

'To marry Luca?' he said softly.

Her hand stilled on the door. 'What else can I do?' she said in a low voice. 'I have nowhere else to go. I have no one but my family.' She swallowed a sob. 'Luca's not so bad, I suppose.'

Finn shook his head in disbelief. ''I can't believe I'm having this conversation with a woman in the late twentieth century,' he said. 'Have you no independence at all?'

She stiffened her body and stared at him. 'Independence?' she echoed, trying to match his tone. 'In my family? How can I be independent? I have no money, I am not qualified to do anything except ...' She waved her hands. 'Except marry, run a home and bring up children.'

She glared at him. 'Maybe if I'd been brought up somewhere else I'd be running an oil company, like in those soaps you see on TV. But I wasn't, and I'm not, and I can't help it.'

He looked at her for a long moment and then lifted his hands helplessly and dropped them. 'I'm sorry,' he said. 'I suppose that was a rather stupid remark.'

Cara relaxed a little at his tone. 'I know that I have led a very sheltered life,' she said carefully. 'But I never saw it as something particularly to regret until I found myself locked into marrying Luca.'

She shrugged self-consciously, 'If I'm honest, at first I liked the idea. I thought of the nice big house we would live in, and I imagined the dinner parties, the clothes ...' Her voice faltered. 'The children I would have.'

She bit her lip and then went on more steadily. 'And then little by little, I realised that in every picture I conjured up, none of them contained Luca.'

She raised her eyes to Finn's. 'Not one,' she repeated. 'Isn't that crazy? It was as if I was just day-dreaming. And then someone, I forget who, someone made a joke about my wedding night, and I realised that I really was going to marry Luca, that it was all set, and that after all the things I had imagined—the ceremony and the fuss and the party—I was actually going to have to get into bed with him.'

Her voice trailed away and she swallowed. 'You probably think this was really silly of me, that it took so long to come to grips with reality. But Luca has always been in my life. I just never thought of him as a husband.'

Her eyes rested briefly on Finn's face and then slid away while she waited for him to tell her how stupid she had been. Why on earth had she told him all that? He was a stranger who at best probably thought she was as dim as Luca did. She oughtn't to be telling him anything.

It was with a bolt of pure shock that she felt him take her hand and raise it to his lips. 'What...what are you doing?' she blurted.

He kissed her hand and smiled at her. 'Just a spur of the moment thing,' he drawled. 'But it seems kind of appropriate to kiss the person who's belted Luca Finzi right where it hurts.'

She tugged her hand away. 'Well, don't,' she said, more sharply than she meant to. It was just silly, the way he was making her feel. Desperately, she cast around for something to say. Anything.

'If I could choose,' she said hurriedly. 'If I *was* independent, then maybe I would go to England.' She looked him straight in the eye and tried to ignore the way her heart was thumping erratically. 'My nanny was English, and my uncle always used to listen to her. He said Sarah talked a lot of sense. Maybe if I went to her, he would listen again.'

There was a long silence, so long that she looked away and began to wonder if he had lost interest in the whole conversation. Maybe he was waiting for her to get out of the car.

Then he sighed, and she looked quickly at him. 'What's the matter? Don't you think it's a good idea?'

'It stinks,' he said simply.

Her eyes narrowed, but before she could say anything Finn went on, 'Let's get this straight, okay? Just so there's no confusion. We are on the run from the Mafia and you think the only person they will listen to is some decrepit old nanny of yours who probably spends most of her days mumbling over her knitting?'

Cara thought of the last time she had seen Sarah. Even now her nanny wouldn't be more than fifty, and her natural elegance was the kind that drew all eyes. Her jaw dropped at the picture Finn was drawing, but in the circumstances his conclusions were probably reasonable enough. She just had to get him to see her point of view. 'You're being over the top,' she said as calmly as she could.

'Over the top?' he echoed. 'Me? Uh-uh. There's somebody in this car who has a screw loose, and it's certainly not me. Not even a baby would think that your answer to Mary Poppins will be able to wave a magic wand and save you.'

Cara shrugged angrily. 'Take me back to the church, then,' she said recklessly.

He grabbed her other arm and gave her a little shake. 'Are you crazy?'

She glared at him. 'Do what you like,' she snapped. 'I'm perfectly sane. And so is Sarah. She's the only one that stands any chance of making my uncle listen.'

He looked at her scathingly, and she burst out, 'Well, she is! And for your information I don't think she does much knitting.'

'Probably past it,' snapped Finn. 'Isn't there anybody else you know?'

'No one,' Cara said firmly. 'She is our best bet, truly.'

'So why wasn't she at the wedding?' he demanded.

Cara shrugged. 'Uncle Pancrazio said she was too ill to come.'

Finn nodded. 'That figures,' he said drily.

Cara realised she was pleating a small square of her dress. 'Would you lend me the money for a plane ticket to England?' she asked at last, not daring to look up.

'No,' he replied, and her heart sank. 'There's no way you could get on a plane without being spotted and stopped by Luca's men,' he added. 'I'm going to England. I have contacts there who may be of use. I'll take you.'

'In the car?' she said blankly. 'With you? All the way to England?'

He smiled mockingly at her. 'I think you have the gist of the idea.'

'On my own, with you?' she added again, just to be quite certain.

'Of course,' he said casually. 'It would be a business arrangement.'

Her head jerked up and she stared him straight in the face, her pulse suddenly thundering in her ears.

He gazed blandly at her. 'But it would be to our mutual benefit . . . and even enjoyment, I hope.'

She licked dry lips. So that was it. She might have known there was a price attached. 'You want me to...' But she couldn't say it. Couldn't bring herself to put into words what Finn might be suggesting.

His fingers brushed her cheek. Her voice when it came seemed very old and far away. 'Go to hell,' she told him.

His fingers paused, then he tipped her face to his, his eyes darkening as he took in her exasperation. 'I do believe,' he drawled, 'that you think I'm expecting you to go to bed with me.'

Her heart was jumping so much she felt like it was bouncing into her throat. 'What other kind of a proposition would a man like you make?' she asked.

His hand slid around the back of her neck and drew her closer. 'Would you accept?' he asked.

She sat upright, her nerves twanging at his tone and his touch. 'What do you think I am?' she asked miserably.

'The question is,' he corrected softly, 'what do you think *you* are? Since the idea of you paying your way by going to bed with me wasn't actually what I had in mind.'

A slow flush crept up her skin at his words, flooding her throat and then her face until she was crimson. 'It never occurred to me that a man like you could have any other sort of proposition in mind,' she said as bitingly as she could.

'Well, if you're willing to consider it, I am,' he drawled. 'What exactly did you have in mind? Instalment payments?'

Her hand made a sharp cracking sound on his cheek before she had consciously thought of retaliating.

But before she could withdraw her hand his fingers enclosed her wrist and he was staring at her, his eyes inky pools. 'You count yourself so little,' he said harshly. 'And other people even less. Do you really think I am the kind of man who would blackmail a woman into bed?'

The look in his eyes was too searing, too probing. She twisted away from him and looked in silence at the woods. 'I don't know what kind of a man you are,' she admitted at last. 'Except that you must be crazy to be helping me like this.'

'Did your family make you this suspicious?' he asked softly. 'This jumpy?'

'It's none of your business,' she replied. 'I don't want to talk about it.'

She knew without looking that he was leaning towards her, moving close. Too close for comfort. She pressed herself against the door and turned to face him. 'Don't touch me!' she yelled in sudden panic. 'Don't you dare!'

'What would you do if I did?' he demanded. 'Have a fit of the vapours?'

She gasped as if he had slapped her, but he continued, 'Don't you want to know what I was going to suggest? Or are you planning on running up that road all on your own? Because I guarantee you won't get very far.'

She tore her eyes away from him and stared at her hands. 'What was your proposition?' she asked in a small voice.

'I want some inside information about your family,' he said. 'I'm writing a new book, and you're perfectly placed to tell me all sorts of things I would never be able to find out otherwise.'

Her heart sank. 'You're barking up the wrong tree,' she said dully. 'I keep telling you. You've got it all wrong about my family.'

He shrugged. 'I'm willing to take the risk,' he said. 'Provided you tell me what you know.'

'But I don't know anything,' she burst out. 'Truly.'

He shrugged. 'Then I'm the loser. But I'm willing to take that chance. I'll take you to England, and when we get there you can tell me what you know. Is it a deal?'

She lifted her hands helplessly. 'You're just...'

'Is it a deal?' he repeated.

Cara dropped her hands and sighed. 'How long do you think the journey will take?' she asked.

He shrugged. 'Three, maybe four days. Maybe less.'

Four days on her own with a man she had never met before. She looked into his blue, blue eyes and felt herself beginning to flush a deep red. 'It's...impossible,' she said. 'I don't even know if I can trust you.'

For one split second he looked absolutely exasperated, then he calmly leant over her once more and pushed the door open. 'Give my love to Luca, won't you?'

CHAPTER TWO

CARA looked at the woods, sunk in shadowy silence, the
sun glinting through the trees, then at Finn. 'I don't have
much choice, do I?' she asked softly.

'You made your choice back there in the church,' he
said quietly. 'Now you have to decide whether to go on
or back down.'

She gazed steadily into his face, the nodded. 'Okay,'
she said as decisively as she could. 'I'll come.'

'Attagirl.' He smiled encouragingly, and to her astonishment she felt herself beginning to smile back.

'Right, come on,' he said briskly. 'Out of the car.'

'Out?' she echoed. 'But we're in the middle of nowhere!' Suddenly she looked at him with new eyes, their
previous conversation doing nothing to stop the panic
spattering through her veins. 'What are you going to
do?' she whispered. 'You're not—'

'A part-time rapist?' he supplied softly, a look in his
eyes she couldn't quite interpret. 'Or maybe a mad axe
murderer?' He shook his head. 'No, these days I seem
to get my kicks out of ruining Mafia weddings.'

'My family hasn't got anything to do with the Mafia,'
she said hotly. 'I keep telling you.'

Finn looked disinterestedly out the window. 'If you
say so,' he said calmly. 'Maybe I've got this all wrong,
after all. Maybe I should just drop you off here. And
then you can go home, explain everything in that won-
derfully persuasive way you have, and everything'll be
hunky-dory.

'Your uncle will be terribly understanding, of course, and Luca...' He paused. 'Well, Luca will probably just have a couple of aspirin and a lie-down in a darkened room and then forget all about it.'

'Leave my family out of this,' she snapped.

He leant towards her. 'Honey, I would love to leave your family out of this. But I don't think that's quite what they have in mind. The sooner we get to England and I get some protection for you, the better.'

Their eyes locked, and Carenza bit her lip. 'Why do you want me to get out of the car?' she asked steadily.

'Because we need to do something about that dress,' he replied. 'It's just the tiniest bit of a giveaway, don't you think?'

She stared at Finn for a long moment, her thudding pulse subsiding. Then with an effort she nodded and got out of the car. She stood by the door, uncertain, watchful as he got out on his side with an easy grace.

There was something about him that drew the eye, that made her want to look at nothing else, but when he turned and glanced at her over the top of the car, she felt herself beginning inexplicably to blush.

He was coming around to her side, and she turned to meet him, beginning to attempt a smile and then instinctively freezing as she noticed the knife in his hand.

He waggled it at her and she stepped back, wondering whether she should try to run. The strange thing was, she didn't feel frightened of him. But maybe he really was a crazy man. Madmen often seemed charming, didn't they? Perhaps he was someone with violent delusions. She took another step back and felt the car hard against her.

'What…what are you doing?' Her voice was wobbly, but she couldn't help it. She forced herself to lift her chin and look him straight in the eye.

'Here,' he said impatiently, turning the knife around and handing it to her, handle first. 'Take it.'

She looked at it blankly as her fingers curled around it, noting mechanically as the tension eased out of her body that it was just an ordinary penknife, and then stared at him. 'What do you want me to do with it?' she asked.

He moved his hands irritably. 'I don't know,' he retorted. 'But you have to do something with that dress of yours. Cut those frilly bits off, cut it shorter, anything. I don't care, but make it look more like a normal dress.'

She gazed at the creased white silk and then at him. 'I can't cut this up,' she whispered. 'It's a work of art. It was made by Elsa Schiapparelli in nineteen thirty something. The hand-stitching alone—'

His jaw clenched and he took a step towards her. 'I don't care if it was made by Elsa the lion in *Born Free*, just do something with it!'

She looked into his lean, lightly tanned face and bit her lip. 'Maybe I could borrow some of your clothes,' she said at last.

He slapped his forehead with his hand. 'You know,' he said softly, 'I thought I had everything for this trip. The penknife that has so many attachments I'm sure there's a fold-up bicycle among them, an idiot-proof camera, a well-respected credit card. And you know what? I left all my dresses at home. Isn't that extraordinary?'

Cara ripped the flowers from her hair and threw them on the ground. She wanted to stamp on them, she was so suddenly, furiously angry. 'You are the most impossible man I have ever met,' she stormed. 'You just walk in and steal me from my wedding as though you had ice water in your veins, and now you are acting like an outraged duchess at the idea of me wearing one of your shirts.'

Finn's mouth opened and then closed with a snap. Without another word he yanked open the boot and tore out a grip. 'Okay,' he said. 'So sometimes you're allowed to have better ideas than me. But we've wasted enough time. It'll be dark soon, and I want to get moving.' He smiled. 'I keep thinking I hear a fleet of Mercedes thundering up the road, with Luca at the head doing his impersonation of Vlad the Impaler.'

A thin chill went down her spine as she thought of how terrifying Luca could be when he was angry. She looked straight into Finn's face.

'What's the matter?' he demanded.

'You don't look particularly scared at the idea of being chased by Luca,' she said softly.

He shrugged. 'He hasn't caught me yet,' he replied quietly. 'And in any case, I'm more worried about you.' He looked at the sky and then at her. 'At least I stand no chance of him deciding to marry me.'

'It's not funny,' she said shortly.

'I'm not laughing,' he replied. 'But I'd appreciate it if you got a move on.'

Cara stepped towards him, then turned around. In a voice as impersonal as she could make it, she said, 'You'll have to undo me. I can't reach all the catches.'

There was a short sigh and then silence, but she knew that he was standing right behind her. It wasn't the feel of his body heat, or the soft brush of his breath on the nape of her neck, but something about his presence she simply couldn't explain. Something she had never before experienced. And as his fingers began to free each cunningly hidden hook and eye, fleetingly touching her skin, she drew in a sharp breath.

'What's the matter?' he asked softly, 'did I stick a pin in you by mistake?'

'No,' she replied unsteadily.

'There,' he said, his voice almost too controlled as he freed the last hook.

She turned quickly. 'Finn—' She was so close to him, he was almost embracing her. 'Why...' She swallowed. 'Why are you doing this, really? Why did you step in like that?'

He said nothing, but his arms closed about her, and he held her hazel eyes with his. It seemed the most natural thing in the world to rest the palms of her hands on his shirt. She could feel the play of his muscles under the cotton, and wondered what his chest looked like without... She shook her head. This was ridiculous. Why couldn't she get a grip on reality? It must be some sort of emotional reaction to everything that had happened, she thought. But she didn't pull away. Somehow, inexplicably, she didn't want to.

His fingers brushed her cheek. 'You are a very beautiful woman, Cara,' he said softly.

'That's not an answer,' she accused, determined to hang on to the last shreds of her self-control, in spite of the fact that it felt so right, so comforting, to be held by him.

There were a few faint freckles on his high cheekbones. 'What sort of answer would you like?' he murmured, taking the pins from her carefully styled dark gold hair and watching it cascade thickly down her back.

'A sensible answer,' she said, trying hard and failing to look away.

'Like this?' he asked, as he bent his head and kissed her.

Her body tautened at the feel of his lips on hers, coaxing, flattering, not at all like Luca's. She pulled away at that thought, but Finn's hands were warm on her back and, astonished at herself, she relaxed.

His lips pressed harder, became more demanding, his fingers trailing down her spine, and Cara reached up to touch his hair, the palm of her hand sliding over his jaw, the faint roughness of his cheek. This was an experience she wanted to go on forever.

And then he stopped. His hands dropped to his sides and he looked at her and smiled grimly. 'Some wedding this is turning out to be.'

It was as if he had broken a spell. Her face flaming, she pulled back, and he let her go. 'I don't know why I let you do that,' she snapped, snatching away her hands.

His fingers imprisoned one of her wrists and he lifted it to his mouth, kissing the pulse point, holding her once more with his eyes.

'Let me go,' she demanded, knowing he could feel the blood thundering through her veins.

'I wouldn't move too fast if I were you, princess,' he remarked. 'That dress is staying up now by sheer willpower.'

'I said, let me go,' she snarled.

With a little smile he dropped her hand, and after a mock bow, he turned and walked to the edge of the trees.

Cara breathed out in one gusty sigh. Making sure he had his back to her, she let the dress drop to her feet. She ran to his suitcase, her high heels wobbling perilously in the soft earth. With a muttered oath, she kicked them off, knelt and flipped the catches on the case, then began rummaging desperately through his clothes.

'There's a Hawaiian shirt and a pair of shorts at the bottom,' said Finn.

She looked up to find him staring at her. 'Go away!' she screamed.

'Cara,' he said gently. 'We're not exactly in the fitting rooms of Saks Fifth Avenue. Get the damned clothes and get in the car.' Blushing furiously, she did as he said, pulling on the shirt and running to the passenger seat as he stuffed the dress, the wreath and her shoes into his case.

'Attagirl,' he said, sliding into the driving seat and taking a good look around. 'Just getting dusk now. It'll be fully dark in a few minutes, and with luck no one will notice us at all on the *autostrada*.'

Cara stared at him, the memory of what they had done suddenly becoming horribly real. 'Luca's men will see us get on,' she whispered. 'They'll be watching for us when we go through the toll booth.'

He glanced at her. 'We're not going through the toll booth,' he said at last, starting the car and driving onto the road.

'But there is no other way,' she objected.

Finn shook his head. 'This road leads to the construction site for the new section of the *autostrada*,' he said equably. 'I was looking at it yesterday, funnily enough, and it's just about completed. We just get on it, drive along till we hit the main *autostrada* and then, *voilà*.'

'Are you French?' she asked after a short pause, thinking for the first time of that strange lilt to his otherwise perfect English. 'Because you are certainly mad.'

'Irish American, actually,' he said mildly.

'Even worse,' she replied glumly, shrugging irritably as he glanced sidewise at her.

'Have you any better ideas?' he inquired.

She shook her head.

'Well, then,' he said. 'At least this one has the advantage of surprise. No one will be expecting us to use this route, and when we get on the *autostrada* we just keep on it till we hit the French border.'

'Uncle Pancrazio is a very powerful man,' she told him. 'And so is Luca. They have contacts everywhere, and they're not going to stop until they find us.'

'You think we should give up?' Finn asked softly.

Cara clasped her hands together tightly. 'I don't know why you stepped in like that this afternoon,' she began. 'I don't believe it was anything to do with your stupid book. But maybe you should just drop me off here and get away on your own. The risk is too great for you. I ... I'll go back to my family and apologise.'

'And marry Luca,' Finn added softly.

'He probably won't want me now,' she said shakily. 'Anyway, I can stand up for myself. Don't bother about me.'

Finn screeched to a stop among the piled-up building materials on the road site. Cara put her hands out to stop herself from hitting the windscreen, then looked at him. 'What did you do that for?' she demanded.

Finn was glaring at her, and she sat up straight. 'Well?' she asked, trying hard and failing to stare him down.

'If you think I went through all that this afternoon just so you could turn yourself into some sort of sacrificial virgin on my behalf,' he snarled, 'you better think again.'

'It's the only reasonable way out,' she said furiously. 'All this talk of escape to England is just so much hot air. There's no way they're not going to catch us.'

He stared hard at her. 'Just tell me, once and for all,' he said grimly. 'Do you or do you not want to marry Luca?'

Cara moved her hands impatiently, pleadingly. 'Of course I don't want to marry him. I told you the truth. I just got led along by degrees until I found myself right on the edge of the chasm. But the price you'll pay for pulling me back is too great.'

'What do you think your family will do if they catch us?' His voice was soft, almost conversational, as if he was discussing the outcome of a local election.

She looked at her lap. 'I don't know,' she said dully.

He reached over and tipped her chin. 'Cara, that's the first time you've tried to lie to me, and you're not very good at it. We both know that we've gone too far to back down. If you went back now, your life wouldn't be worth living.'

'At least I would be alive,' she replied bitterly. 'You have to get away. You've risked enough.'

A slow smile spread over his face as he looked at her.

'What?' she demanded. 'What are you smiling at?'

'You,' he replied, putting the car into gear and beginning towards the distant ribbon of lights that marked the *autostrada*. 'You're a very brave woman, Cara, but I think I'll take a rain check on your offer.'

'It's no use arguing with you, is it?' she asked softly.

'No,' he replied. 'Not this time. And do me a favour, will you?'

'What?' she asked.

He flicked her a glance. 'Do up your damn seat belt before I have a nervous breakdown.'

It was almost fully dark, and there was no moon. Cara pulled off her tights and pulled on Finn's shorts. They were impossibly big on her, but with luck the shirt would hide the bagginess. She glanced at Finn, tensing as he slowed down.

'What's the matter?' she asked.

'There are cars guarding the slip road,' he said. 'Your family is more thorough than I gave them credit for.' He glanced at her and squeezed her hand. 'But maybe we can still get through. Get in the back, on the floor.'

Without a word, she did as he said. Finn drove steadily towards Luca's men. He wound down the window, and she held her breath. There were shouts and then Finn answered. 'Would you believe it,' he yelled in perfect Italian. 'Three pairs of lovers on this stretch of God-forsaken road, and none of them were our birds. I'm going to take a turn on the *autostrada*, see if they've managed to escape the net.'

Cara lay on the floor behind his seat, her fists clenched, waiting for the angry shouts to come, the gunshots, willing Finn to accelerate, get the hell out of this crazy place. But he just kept going smoothly on.

'It's all right,' he said at last, slipping into English as if it were the most natural way in the world to speak to her. 'You can come out now.'

Warily she risked a quick look out the window. She could see nothing except the swift passing lights of cars. They were on the *autostrada*. Stiffly she got up and climbed into the front seat. 'You have the luck of...' She shrugged helplessly.

'The Irish?' he supplied, smiling into the darkness.

'Of the devil!' she retorted.

'Why are you so cross?' he asked mildly.

'I am not cross!' she snapped.

'Of course not.'

There was silence, and she looked at the cars going by. For the moment, at least, she was free.

'You could have got yourself killed back there,' she said at last.

He shrugged. 'Perhaps. But there are worse fates.'

She stared at him wonderingly. 'Such as?'

He cocked a glance at her, then stared at the road. 'Such as marrying Luca Finzi,' he said quietly.

It had been dark for hours, but it was still hot and it had not taken Cara long to discover that Finn's hire car had no air-conditioning.

The stale, warm fumes blowing in through her window from the traffic were giving her a headache. She had a cramp in her right foot, which no amount of rubbing would get rid of. And every few moments she had to look over her shoulder, as if somehow she could pick out Luca's car from all the others.

'Relax,' soothed Finn. 'It's highly unlikely they know what kind of car we have, or the registration. They don't even know for certain that we're on the *autostrada* or what direction we're going in.'

Cara bit her lip. 'I may be naïve, Finn, but I'm not stupid. They're bound to have figured out by now that it was you on the slip road. And you know as well as I that they can't be far behind.'

She looked at his strong profile in alternate shade and light from the other cars. 'Tell me the truth,' she said quietly. 'What odds do you give for our success?'

He sighed. 'I'd rather give odds on a dead horse winning the Kentucky Derby, if you want the truth,' he said at last. 'But we're not done yet.'

They both looked in silence at the road ahead, then Finn glanced at her. 'It's not entirely hopeless, you know,' he said. 'At this precise moment, we're free.'

'You always were free,' she replied softly. 'You didn't have to rescue me.'

He didn't reply to that, and Cara wondered again if some ulterior motive had prompted him to come to her aid. There had to be one. He couldn't have done it just for the sake of a book. Money, maybe? Had some other family decided the marriage would make Luca and her uncle a too-powerful combination and paid Finn to step in?

She thought of the look in Finn's eyes when he had taken her hand in the church and sighed. Somehow she didn't like to think he had accepted money to take her away. And besides, nobody, not even she, had known she would rebel like that at the last moment.

Maybe he was just crazy. After all, who in his right mind would bring out a book like that about Luca and then attend his wedding?

And why would a complete stranger help her for her own sake? And how did he know she spoke English?

Finn's voice broke in on her thoughts. 'You're thinking so loudly it's disturbing me,' he remarked. 'What's bugging you now?

She swallowed. 'I was wondering if you were safe to be with,' she said frankly. 'Because I am beginning to think you are certainly not right in the head.'

He shrugged. 'Can you think of anybody in your family who is completely sane?' he inquired. 'Your uncle, for instance—'

'Leave my uncle out of it!' she broke in hotly.

'All right,' Finn went on. 'Luca, then. Now there is a man who is definitely one plate short of a picnic basket. He is so macho your uncle probably keeps him on a leash and feeds him the remains of door-to-door salesmen.'

Cara stared at him. No one had ever spoken so casually about her family before. So insultingly. 'How dare you!' she fumed.

He turned to look at her briefly. 'Okay, so I was exaggerating, but so what? The trouble with you, Cara, is that you've been brought up to accept unquestioningly everything your uncle and Luca tell you.'

Her mouth opened but she could think of nothing to say.

He went on. 'I've studied the way your family does business for a long time. And I thought nothing could surprise me about them any more. But I have to admit I was as surprised as Luca when you turned at the altar and just said no. He looked like a guy whose pet rabbit had just pulled a gun on him.'

Cara's jaw clenched. 'So you think I'm just a pet rabbit?'

He held up his hand. 'Uh-uh.' He shook his head. 'When you arrived at the church I thought you were a sacrificial lamb. Now...' He put his hand on the steering wheel. 'Now, I don't know what to make of you. Except that you're probably as crazy as you think I am.'

She stared out the windscreen. Sacrificial lamb, indeed. Just who did this man think he was?

He glanced at her. 'You must be tired,' he said matter-of-factly. 'Try to sleep.'

'I don't want to,' she snapped. And was immediately angry with herself for how childish she sounded. She

rubbed her hands over her face and tried to stifle a yawn.
'I can't sleep. I still don't even know if I can trust you
or not.'

'I'm the only hope you've got,' he said drily. 'And,
in any case, what do you think I'm going to do—try to
rape you with one foot on the accelerator? Interesting
idea,' he added meditatively. 'Especially on the
autostrada. But I have to admit I'm not that much of
an acrobat.'

She leaned her head back. He really had the most
beautiful voice, she thought sleepily. But the things he
said with it! She had never, ever met a man like him.

Soon she fell into an uneasy doze, peopled with unsettling images. Finn glanced at her face, and with a wry
smile kept on driving.

She woke with a start as he pulled into a service station.
'Where are we?' she asked muzzily.

'Past Rome,' he replied. 'Nearly at Florence. 'It's
about two o'clock, and if we keep this up, we should be
in France for lunch tomorrow.'

Lunch. Her brain seemed to wake up all of a sudden
at the word, and she tried to remember when she had
last eaten. She looked at him hopefully. 'I don't suppose
we could have something to eat now?' she ventured.

'I'll see what I can do,' he said, getting out of the car.
'Keep your head down.'

Cara looked at the parking area in front of the shop
and restaurant. Even at this hour in the morning it was
busy. And noisy. The people were mostly families and
some young couples, all eating snacks and laughing in
the velvet darkness. There was no danger here. Nobody
looked like one of Luca's men.

But it was still difficult not to feel scared. Not to wonder if even now Luca was pulling up behind them and getting out of his car... She shook herself crossly. She mustn't think like that. She couldn't afford to panic.

Sliding down in her seat, Cara noticed a briefcase on the floor. She must have knocked it off the back seat when Finn was smuggling her past Luca's men. She grabbed the handle to heft it up, but the catch hadn't been fastened, and a bundle of papers cascaded over the floor.

Muttering crossly under her breath she began to pick them up, and then stopped, amazed, as she read her name.

The papers were cuttings, from English newspapers, and she frowned in concentration as she began to read. Talking to Finn had brought everything she had forgotten flooding back.

Including some things, maybe, that were best left untouched in her memory, like Sarah and her uncle having that enormous row when she had been about eleven. Sarah had left shortly after that. All that had been left were a few classic novels with Sarah's name written on the flyleaf. Occasionally Cara read them, but only occasionally. The clean, expensive smell of the thick cream pages was enough to bring back the memory of a woman she had once hoped would become her stepmother. And who instead had disappeared out of her life for ever.

'Carenza Gambini.' She stared in amazement at her printed name, her mind focusing once more on the present. What was she doing in a newspaper? 'The beautiful but obviously gormless niece of one of the Mafia's greatest mobsters is set to marry the equally ruthless Luca Finzi. She better get his breakfast eggs just right, or Lucky, as he is so imaginatively known, will probably be signing quite another contract for her. Until death do they part...'

Cara's heart pounded as she read the piece over and over again. Is this what people all over England had read about her? There was a crunch of gravel by the car and she looked up, straight into Finn's eyes.

'And may I ask why you're rummaging around in my briefcase?' he demanded.

She held the cutting out to him with shaking fingers. 'Did you have anything to do with this?' she demanded.

He looked straight into her eyes. 'I wrote it.'

'You wrote it!' she screeched. 'It's rubbish!'

He shrugged. 'It pays.'

She pushed against the door. 'Let me out of the car,' she snapped.

'What are you going to do?' he drawled. 'Stick me with a hairpin?'

'Let me out!' she repeated.

'It's all gravel out here,' he said. 'You'll hurt your feet.'

She glared at him. 'I want to hurt you!'

He shifted his weight and opened the door. She swung her legs out of the car. He was right, it was gravel. Determinedly she stood to face him, then grabbed at her shorts as they fell down.

'You could use your tights as a belt,' Finn offered.

'Don't give me advice,' she snarled. 'How many other lies have you written about me?'

He rubbed his chin. 'I don't know. After meeting you I'm not sure what the truth is any more.'

Crossly she stamped her foot on the gravel and stifled a yelp of pain. 'How dare you call me gormless!'

'It was a logical assumption,' he replied calmly. 'Given that you had just agreed to marry Luca.'

She pulled out another cutting and waved it in his face. 'And this!' she yelled. 'This one claims I spend all my time shopping!'

'Don't you?' he asked, interested.

She drew in her breath sharply and glared at him. 'I'm going to the ladies',' she snapped, and before he could do anything she had spun round and scuttled barefoot to the main building, the gravel like hot coals on her feet.

In the ladies' her face looked like a ghost's in the brightly lit wall of mirrors. She rubbed hastily at her cheeks with a dampened paper towel. With almost savage satisfaction she wiped off the too-bright lipstick and the thick mascara the professional make-up girl had insisted on.

That had been for the wedding pictures, she had been told. She had hated it, but naturally enough, her opinion had not been taken into account. She ran her fingers through her disordered hair and rinsed her mouth.

Strange, really, that she should belong to such a thoroughly Italian family and yet look nothing like them. Thick gold hair, pale skin that, if she wasn't careful, burnt before it tanned, and those wide hazel eyes.

Her father had been like that, too, her uncle had said. A throwback to Roman times, he had told her, laughing. But her parents had died when she was a baby, and the photographs she had of them were blurred and mostly out of focus.

Perhaps Finn could tell her more. She had never seen the book he had written about Luca. She had just accepted that it was a lie. Money-grubbing filth, as Luca had put it. Now she began to think she would very much like to read it.

Washing her face and hands in cool water was heaven after that long, hot drive. She soaked another paper towel and bathed the back of her neck, then, shrugging helplessly at her reflection, went outside.

The car was not where Finn had parked it. She registered the fact almost unconsciously, and then as she realised the implications her heart flopped sickeningly.

He had left her. Deserted her. She stared at the spot where the car had been, then looked wildly around. Had he really gone?

She almost screamed when a hand descended on her shoulder and spun her round. 'Where the hell have you been?' Finn snapped.

She gazed at him in shock. 'I . . . I told you, I went to the ladies',' she replied as calmly as she could.

'On which planet?' he demanded. 'Do you know how long you've been? I could have filled up ten cars at that gas station in the time it's taken you to mess about in there.'

She glared at him, anger replacing her fear. 'What's it to you?' she retorted.

CHAPTER THREE

FINN grabbed her wrist and pulled her to him. 'We are not on some Sunday jaunt,' he said quietly, emphasising every word. 'This is a dangerous game you've started, and it doesn't pay to play around with your relatives. Didn't it ever occur to you that I might think the worst when you didn't immediately come back?'

She stared into his eyes. 'I know more about my relatives than you do,' she told him.

'I doubt it,' he drawled.

'You are so arrogant,' she said at last. 'You always think you know best. Don't you? I bet the only reason you were angry when I didn't come back was because you thought the source for your latest book had just gone west.'

He stared, and she dropped her eyes. Then he sighed and released her.

She stood back, rubbing her wrist as though he had hurt her, and he shrugged irritably and pushed his fingers through his hair. A lock of it, like an untidy comma, fell over his forehead, and she stifled an entirely unreasonable instinct to reach up and brush it back.

'You can leave right now, if you want to,' he said softly.

She glared at him, reddening, knowing he was aware of the way she had been staring at him. 'You know I can't,' she answered. 'That's a rotten thing to say to me.'

'Maybe,' he agreed, his eyes as hard as ice on a cold night. 'But then I'm a rotten kind of person.' He turned on his heel and walked away, and after a few seething seconds Cara stalked after him, her teeth clenched as the gravel bit into her feet.

The car was parked in darkness near the exit, and she watched silently as Finn unlocked it. And then her eyes slid away from his angry eyes and taut face, seeing without registering at first a dark blue car coasting into the garage forecourt.

A very familiar dark blue car, empty except for one man. Luca.

'Finn,' she breathed, unable to say any more, the hairs lifting on the back of her neck.

Luca was easing his bulk out of the car. Then, halfway out, he saw her.

She stood stock-still, staring at him, as he slammed the door and came towards them with all the horrible inevitability of a runaway tank.

Finn spun round. 'Get in the car,' he ordered.

She put a shaking hand on his arm. 'No,' she pleaded. 'Maybe he will listen to me.'

'Cara.' Finn bit the words out. 'In case you hadn't noticed, that is a gun in his hand, and he doesn't look too pleased to see you. Now, get in the car.'

She looked at Luca's hand, the sodium lights of the service station glinting dully off the absurdly small object he was carrying, and stood up straighter. 'I'd rather face him,' she said, her voice sounding strangely high.

Finn reached for her arm and squeezed it. 'Everything's going to be all right, Cara,' he said quietly. 'Just get into the driving seat and start the engine.'

She looked at him, his eyes once more on Luca, then did as she was told.

Finn, too, got into the car and pulled the door closed just as Luca came to a stop about three feet from them.

'I should kill you where you sit,' the Italian said. 'Both of you.'

'Bit messy,' Finn remarked, his hand inside a paper sack he picked from the floor. 'And besides—' he shrugged '—what's to say I won't shoot first?'

He lifted his hand out of the bag, and the Italian glanced in surprise at the pistol Finn was holding. 'You wouldn't dare shoot,' he blustered. 'I have men all around.'

'Not true,' said Finn conversationally. 'On both counts.' He waggled the gun at Luca and added, 'If you shoot me, I'll shoot you, and that won't get either of us anywhere. I'd go away and get some reinforcements if I were you.'

Cara swallowed hard. She had never heard anyone talk to Luca like that before. And yet Finn seemed so relaxed about it. As if he really didn't care whether he upset him or not.

She stared straight ahead, looking out of the corner of her eye at the people crowded around the restaurant. So far they seemed oblivious to what was going on, but she wondered if Luca would do anything in such a public place.

He was glaring at them as if he was thinking about what Finn had said. 'You wouldn't dare shoot me,' he repeated at last.

'Try me,' replied Finn. He added in an undertone to Cara, 'Get going, for God's sake.' With one terrified glance at Luca she pressed her foot down on the accelerator, and the car leapt away spitting gravel. There were two sharp noises, as if a car had backfired, then they were on the *autostrada* once more.

'He shot at us,' gasped Cara, changing gear and forgetting to put the clutch down. 'He actually shot at us.'

'Yes,' replied Finn shortly. 'Still think you can persuade him to see reason?'

'You had a gun, too,' she retorted. 'That makes you just as bad as the rest of them.'

He looked at what he was carrying and smiled. 'Not quite.'

There was a pause, then Cara glanced curiously at him. 'Would you have shot him?'

There was an expression on his face she couldn't read at all. 'What's the matter?' she asked.

He hefted the gun in his hand and gazed at her rather apologetically. 'I don't think this would hurt anyone,' he said at last. 'Although I suppose it could make their teeth fall out.'

She wondered if she was hearing correctly. 'Are you all right?' she asked tentatively. 'Shock can do funny things to people.'

'You think I'm crazy, don't you?' replied Finn, and then her heart stopped as he put the gun in his mouth.

'Mother of God!' she shouted. 'What the hell are you playing at now?' With an enormous effort of will she kept driving. 'Look,' she said as calmly as she could. 'Don't do this. Please. I beg you. I—I'm sorry I said all those things to you back at the service station. Your nerves obviously can't take all the strain. Maybe we should get a doctor or something.'

He removed the gun from his mouth and grinned broadly at her. 'You're really sorry?'

She nodded hastily. 'Absolutely.'

To her utter amazement his smile widened. 'Such a shame the gun is only made of chocolate, isn't it?' he remarked. And then putting the fake gun once more in his mouth he bit off a piece and relaxed in his seat. 'Want a bite?'

Her hands felt wet on the wheel. She rubbed them briskly on her shorts and took several deep breaths. 'No, thank you,' she said shortly.

'I always think it's a shame you can't get chocolate bullets, as well,' he mused, breaking off the trigger and offering it to her.

'What about a chocolate cruise missile, full size, that I could drop on your head?' she retorted, taking the piece without even noticing what she was doing.

'Do you always drive like this?' he inquired.

She glared at him, but before she could say anything he asked interestedly, 'Did you have lessons? Or are you learning as you go along?'

She clenched her jaw. 'One of my uncle's bodyguards taught me.'

'That makes me feel much better,' he said drily. 'I've already aged twenty years this afternoon. By the time you're finished I'll need a wheelchair and an oxygen mask.'

Cara's fingers tightened on the wheel. 'Yes, well, you're not the only one,' she said icily. 'If Luca had known about that gun...' Her voice trailed away, her mind almost refusing to accept what had just happened. 'How could you do that?' she whispered.

He shrugged. 'We didn't really have much choice, did we?' he remarked. 'It was either bluff him or give up.'

'But the gun.' Cara thought of what he had done.

Finn stared expressionlessly out the window. 'You said you were hungry,' he remarked. 'And when I went to get you something, they only had sweets left. It was either the gun or a sherbet lollipop.' He shrugged. 'I bought both, actually, but somehow, when it came to the crunch, I didn't think Luca would feel very threatened by a lollipop.'

Cara shook her head. 'If only he knew,' she said softly.

'He's hardly likely to, though, is he?' said Finn, stretching out in his seat. 'You've eaten practically all the evidence.'

'I was hungry!' she retorted earnestly, and then realising that he was winding her up once more, thumped the steering wheel. 'Do you want to drive?' she demanded.

'No,' he said innocently. 'No. I like being driven at a hundred and twenty miles an hour on an Italian motorway by a beautiful woman eating a chocolate gun.'

She shot a furious glance at him. 'Surely you mean a beautiful but gormless woman,' she snapped.

He lifted his hands in mock appeal. 'I didn't know you then,' he said.

She pressed her foot down harder. 'Well, you're not going to get the chance to know me any better now.'

'Is that because you're going to drive us into the middle of next week?' His hand rested lightly on her arm, and she jumped at the contact. 'Slow down, Cara. We don't need to go this fast.'

She eased back jerkily on the accelerator. He nodded. 'That's better,' he said.

'We could have been killed back there.' She forced the words out.

'But we weren't,' he soothed.

She glanced at him curiously. 'You take enormous risks,' she remarked.

'Calculated ones,' he amended.

'Why did you come to my wedding?' she demanded. 'And how did you get into the church? My uncle was really worried about security.'

'I just walked in,' he said blandly.

'After telling a few whopping lies on the way,' she added.

He looked at her, the laughter showing clearly in his eyes. 'Well, maybe a few,' he agreed.

Cara glanced at him, then concentrated on her driving once more.

'What's the matter?' he inquired. 'Have I grown three heads or something?'

She shook her head. 'It's just that I have never met anyone who can talk their way out of trouble like you can,' she said. 'You just…hypnotise people. Charm them into doing what you want them to.'

'Including you?' he asked softly.

She pursed her lips. 'Certainly not,' she snapped.

'Shame,' he said, and smiled. 'We'd make a marvellous couple.'

Cara glared at him, her heart thumping. 'We would not. And you needn't even think about…that sort of thing. I know your type exactly. You don't know where the truth stops and the lies begin.'

Finn was grinning broadly, damn him. 'I only meant,' he said softly, 'that with your driving and my charm we'd be immune from every traffic policeman in Western Europe.' He turned a deceptively innocent gaze on her. 'What did *you* mean, that sort of thing?'

'Nothing,' she snapped, reddening.

He smiled and reached into his jacket pocket. 'I bought a pair of espadrilles for you at the service station. Should have given them to you earlier, but somehow they slipped my mind. Hope they fit.'

She could think of nothing to say. All geared up for another verbal sparring match, she felt totally unmanned by his thoughtfulness. She stole a couple of glances at him out of the corner of her eye, steered into the slow lane, pulled over and stopped the car. 'Thank you,' she said at last, then added quietly, 'I'm sorry I took so long in the ladies' at the service station. I...I didn't really think about the possible dangers.'

She shrugged helplessly, wanting to explain to him how she felt. Wanting him to know exactly how much his actions had meant to her.

'These people...Luca and my uncle and the rest,' she began. 'They're my family. I didn't expect...I mean, I knew they would be angry, but...' She lifted one hand off the steering wheel and gestured in frustration. 'I never expected them to shoot at us. Never.' She turned her head and looked squarely at Finn. 'I suppose you think I'm very naïve, don't you?'

He sighed. 'Maybe if you hadn't been so naïve, you wouldn't have walked out of your wedding like that,' he said at last. 'If you had known how ruthless Luca could be, you might have been too scared.'

'I was scared,' she said softly.

His hand closed over hers. 'You could be at your reception now,' he said reflectively. 'Drinking champagne.'

Her jaw tightened. 'And having money pinned to my dress,' she said.

He raised his eyebrows.

'It's a custom,' she explained. 'Relatives pin money to the bride's dress.' She rested her free hand on her knee, not even conscious that she was clenching it tightly. 'I suppose the original idea was good. But for me...' She shook her head. 'Men trying to curry favour with my uncle and Luca, competing with everyone else to see who would have pinned the most to me. Patting me like some prizewinning heifer.'

Her voice trailed away, then she resumed. 'I wanted to drop the idea, but Luca wouldn't have it. It was not even as though we needed the money.'

Her hand strayed to her cheek as she remembered the row they had had, the pure shock when he slapped her face. It had been the first time she realised how little her opinions counted with him.

She stared furiously through the windscreen, raging at the memory.

'I've got a book of stamps,' said Finn. 'I could pin that to your shorts, if you like.'

The picture made her suddenly snort with laughter, then to her amazement she felt tears prick her eyelids. 'I'm sorry, 'she sniffed. 'I...'

His hand was still closed over hers. 'It's all right, Cara. Let's trade seats, and I'll do some more driving. You look like you could do with a rest.'

'What about Luca?' she whispered.

'I don't give a stuff about Luca,' he said roughly. 'He's probably face down in the car park wondering if I did fire at him and if he's been hit anywhere vital, like his wallet.'

She slid over the seats as Finn got out and came round to the driving side.

'Try to sleep,' he urged.

'You must be joking,' she said woodenly, feeling that she would never be able to sleep again, but within five minutes her head had slipped down and she had fallen into an uneasy doze once more.

Dawn was breaking when she woke. The sodium lights along the *autostrada* were still on, but they looked weak and ineffective against the pale, streaky sky.

She looked at Finn, and everything that had happened the day before came flooding back with dreadful clarity.

'So you're awake, then,' he offered, glancing at her and smiling.

'What's so funny?' she demanded, running her tongue around her lips and wishing she could clean her teeth.

'Nothing, I guess.' He shrugged. 'It's just that I like the peaceful way you sleep. I bet you were a dormouse in a former life.'

She shot a look at him and stretched against the seat. It was odd, thinking of a man watching her while she was asleep. A man she hardly knew at all.

'Do I snore, or something?' she demanded.

He smiled. 'You were too busy talking to snore.'

She glanced at him, horrified. 'I was not,' she breathed.

He shrugged. 'How would you know? You were asleep. I was the one who had to listen to you.'

'What did I say?' she demanded.

'Well, that's the really irritating part,' he said calmly. 'It was all nonsense. Just mumbled stuff, with people's names occasionally. But nothing you could stuff a gossip column with.'

'What a shame for you,' she retorted.

He cocked a smile at her, then looked at the road. Cara folded her arms crossly. She wished she could get up and walk about instead of having to stay put, watching the countryside roll past.

She had cramp again and the beginnings of a blinding headache. What on earth was she doing in this car?

Stupid question, she told herself crossly. She thought of the alternative and tried to picture it clearly in her mind. She would be married to Luca now. Last night would have been her wedding night. She thought of the way he had looked at her in the church and shivered. No, a night—a life of nights—in Luca's bed was not something she wanted to think about.

She stole a look at Finn's profile as he concentrated on the road ahead.

'Feeling okay?' he inquired.

'Yes,' she lied.

He smiled. 'That's what I like to hear, positive thinking.'

'Have you seen anything of Luca?' she asked, not sure if she wanted to know the answer.

'He's about half a mile behind us,' said Finn.

It took about a second for Finn's matter-of-fact words to sink in.

'He's what!' screeched Cara.

Finn glanced at her. 'You heard,' he said calmly.

She clasped her hands so tightly they hurt. 'Well, what are we going to do?' she demanded, the words tumbling nervously out. 'We have to do something.'

Finn nodded. 'I'm going to make a U-turn.'

Cara's jaw dropped. 'On the *autostrada*?'

'Why not?' asked Finn. 'I took the wrong turn-off for this very purpose, so we could throw him off the scent and get him going towards the Alps while we double back towards the coast.'

She clenched her hands and then ran them distractedly through her hair. 'Why don't we just jump out?' she said bitterly. 'And run all the way to England?'

He glanced in the driving mirror. 'That's Plan B,' he said deadpan.

Cara swallowed, her hands curling round her seat belt and then nervously creeping to her mouth. She knew by the set look on Finn's face that he was deadly earnest. Now was no time for arguments.

'Ever done it before?' she asked as casually as she could.

'Not exactly,' Finn admitted, glancing at her, his eyebrows lifting. 'Why have you got your hands over your eyes?'

'I'm an expert in palmistry,' muttered Cara. 'I wanted to see what the next few seconds hold for me.'

The oncoming lanes of the *autostrada* were empty. Finn drove to a gap in the central reservation, braked and spun the wheel. In a matter of seconds they were driving in entirely the opposite direction.

The entire manoeuvre had taken seconds and worked perfectly, but it was some way down the road before Cara dropped her hands from her face and realised that she had been holding her breath. She stole a little look at Finn and smiled with a great rush of relief.

Finn's eyes, however, were on the car that had been behind them. She followed his gaze as it tried and failed to make the turn, and crashed into the central reservation. It was as though suddenly everything was frozen in time, and then a tiny figure scrambled out of the wreck, just before a thin plume of smoke began spiralling into the bright blue sky.

She stared appalled and then tugged on Finn's sleeve. 'We have to stop,' she said urgently.

'What for?' he demanded, amazed.

'Luca crashed,' she said. 'And it was our fault. We must do something.'

Finn glanced at her and kept on driving. 'That man would have killed us both last night, if it wasn't for the fact that it was too public and he thought he stood a good chance of getting killed himself. He tried to force you to marry him, and he wasn't chasing after us to apologise.' He slid the car to the slow lane and reduced his speed. 'And you want to stop and help him?' His voice was loaded with disbelief and anger. 'You saw him get out of the car. What do you want to do—offer him a lift?'

She said nothing, just twisted her hands in her lap.

'Look, Cara,' he went on a little more gently. 'We couldn't stop, even if we wanted to. And it will be miles before we get the chance to turn around. As it is, we have a golden opportunity to get right away. And I, for one, am going to grab it with both hands. And if you're that interested in Luca's welfare, I don't think he'll have been seriously injured. We both saw him get out. He's probably just trashed the car.'

Cara bit her lip and looked out the window. There was nothing she could think of to say. Her reaction had been a purely reflex one, springing from the horror that they had led another human being into a potentially lethal accident. Now she thought of Luca's mobile phone and the number of men at his command. The accident had bought them time, but probably not much.

She looked at Finn's face and knew without saying anything that he was thinking the same thing. There was no point in saying any more. Going back had been a stupid thing to suggest. Finn, damn him, was right.

The morning sun was glancing off the traffic, and Cara scanned the cars they passed for anything familiar, anything that would show if Luca's men were still close on their trail.

'Relax,' urged Finn.

'I can't,' burst out Cara. 'I feel like I'm in one of those dungeons where the walls move closer and closer together, until I'll just get crushed between them.'

She gazed almost pleadingly at him. 'It seemed so easy to run out of the church with you yesterday afternoon. But now I don't know what to do.'

Finn glanced at her. 'You've taken the first step on the high wire,' he said. 'Now you just have to keep putting one foot in front of the other. And don't, whatever you do, look down.'

'Easy for you to say,' she retorted.

He glanced at her. 'In case you hadn't noticed,' he said calmly, 'we are both in this, up to our necks.'

'I'm running away because it's my life,' insisted Cara. 'You're only here because you want to make money by writing a book about it.' She paused. 'At least, that's what you *claim*,' she snapped. 'You could be anyone.'

'It's a bit late to start worrying about my motives now,' he replied. 'What did you want, a rescue application and two references?'

She glared at him. 'Why not?' she demanded. 'Although from the little I know of you, two is probably on the ambitious side.'

There was a muscle pounding in his cheek, and she knew she had gone too far.

She clasped her hands tightly in the ensuing silence. 'I'm sorry,' she said at last. 'It's just the strain of all this. I've never experienced anything like it before. All my life I've known exactly what every day holds, when I'm going to eat, who I'll probably see, where I'll go. And now...' She shrugged helplessly. 'I don't know anything. If I see any of my family, they'll probably kill me, I haven't the faintest idea where I'm going, or anything really about who you are, and I've had one piece of chocolate in the last twenty-four hours.' She paused. 'I haven't even got any clothes.'

The silly, trivial words hung in the air, and Cara wanted to kick herself in the silence that followed. She had sounded so childish. So whingeing. She sighed unhappily. Finn was obviously not impressed, and she couldn't blame him. But if only he could open up a little more....

He stared out the windscreen, seemingly intent on the road. His words, when they came, were cold and remote. 'Do you want me to drop you at a service station?' he asked.

Her lips parted with shock. Did he really want to get rid of her? Silence hung between them like a thick curtain as she tried to think of all the implications of his question.

'Why?' she demanded at last, trying to hold her voice to the same tone as his. 'Will it make things easier for you?'

He said nothing, just kept staring out the windscreen, and she bit her lip. She was going about everything the wrong way. It was about time she did something right. 'You don't need to answer that,' she said finally. 'I'm sorry. We are both in this up to here.' She brought her hand level with her eyes and then looked at him. 'You were right,' she added softly. 'I can only go on and not look down.'

Finn glanced at her, nodding almost imperceptibly, then put all his concentration on the road. But Cara couldn't draw her eyes from him, staring almost unconsciously at the high cheekbones and the full, wide lips.

There were lines of strain there that she had not noticed before, and she clasped one of her hands with the other to stop herself from reaching out to touch his face. It was strange how attracted she felt towards him, the silly things that she wanted to do when she was with him, that she had never in the least felt like doing with Luca.

She could read him, too, that was the odd thing. It was like a message in her brain, telling her that he was aware of her, that he knew she was staring at him even though he was concentrating on his driving. He was smiling, and she felt herself begin to flush. She swallowed and looked away. 'Why did you risk your life to rescue me?' she asked, trying hard to sound objective, disinterested.

He glanced sideways at her, his smile all too apparent, damn him. 'Some people bungee jump off bridges, others roller skate down the Eiffel Tower. Me,' he drawled, 'I like busting up Mafia weddings.'

She shook her head. 'Tell me why, really,' she persisted, unable any longer to keep the pleading out of her voice.

There was silence, a pause so long she thought he was ignoring her. And then he spoke. 'Because I don't like seeing people being pushed around,' he said shortly. 'If you had wanted to get married to the biggest bastard this side of the Alps, that was your business. But when you said no and everyone just ignored you...'

He stopped and shrugged. 'It was something in your face, I guess,' he added. 'I don't know what.' He looked grimly at her. 'That's it, okay? Don't ask me any more damn fool questions. I've got plenty of other things to think about. And so have you.'

On and on they drove, until they came to the end of the *autostrada* and the toll booths just before the French border loomed in front of them. 'You have to have a ticket from where you got on so they know how much to charge you,' said Cara worriedly. 'And we haven't got one.'

'There's plenty of other things to worry about besides lost tickets,' replied Finn calmly, smiling at the woman in the booth and persuading her with devastating charm in his perfect Italian that the *signora*, frowning irritably at Cara, had thrown the ticket, the precious ticket out the window during a row near Bologna.

Five minutes later, having shovelled over an impressive wad of cash and filled up with petrol, they were bowling along on their way.

'I'm afraid you'll have to get down in the back again before we reach the border post,' Finn told her.

'What do you mean?' Cara asked blankly.

He glanced at her, then said drily, 'I'm assuming you didn't pack your passport when you got all done up for your wedding.' He shrugged. 'Of course, I could be wrong.'

'Of course I haven't got my passport with me,' she said crossly. 'But we're in the European Union, in case you hadn't noticed. Nobody bothers with passports any more.'

He looked at her. 'There's still a border, Cara. I agree, they're unlikely to search the car, and we wouldn't last a minute if they did. But I don't really want to get into any arguments about why you haven't got an ID.'

'They'll notice me lying down,' pointed out Cara practically. 'Shouldn't I get in the boot?'

He smiled. 'Don't you think it'll be the tiniest bit attention-grabbing if people see us stopping on the hard shoulder and you climbing into the boot?'

She twisted in her seat to face him as fully as she could. 'Why didn't you think of all this before?' she demanded crossly.

He shrugged. 'I can't think of everything.'

She compressed her lips and stared out the window.

'Cara,' he coaxed. 'It's no big deal. Last time I came this way I just sailed past at sixty miles an hour. And this way, it's one less clue to your whereabouts.'

He was probably right, she thought grudgingly as she stared at his profile. And he had got her this far. With a sigh she unclicked her safety belt and climbed once more into the back and pulled a blanket over her. 'This is silly,' she said, her heart beginning to hammer unreasonably. 'Not even a child could be fooled by this.'

Finn didn't answer, and she lay down, listening to the rumble of the wheels beneath her head. What had she got herself into?

The car slowed fractionally, then picked up speed again. 'Can I come out now?' she demanded after what seemed like several hours but was probably only a few minutes.

'Yes. Be quick,' he replied.

She clambered unsteadily into the front seat and did up her safety belt. 'I hate this car,' she grumbled.

'Welcome to France,' Finn replied, then grinned at her. 'They didn't even want us to stop,' he said. 'I couldn't believe how easy it was.'

She stared at him. 'So you did have your doubts?'

He shrugged. 'It was a risk we had to take,' he said. 'But yes,' he added. 'I did worry a bit.'

'Worry?' she repeated scathingly. 'I'd like to see you worry about something.'

CHAPTER FOUR

FINN glanced at her. 'I worry all the time,' he said easily.

'About what?' she demanded. 'You met Luca last night and you didn't seem to turn a hair. Do you know what bad dreams I had about that incident?'

'Yes,' he replied simply. 'I had a ringside seat, remember?'

She could feel herself flushing again and she gripped her seat belt tightly. 'You told me I wasn't making any sense,' she said stiffly, angry in her embarrassment. She paused and glared at him. 'What did I say this time? Anything interesting for your gossip column?'

He shook his head. 'You didn't say anything, really,' he said. He shot her a look that she couldn't read at all. 'You mumbled a bit, then you shouted out several times. Mostly the word no.' He glanced in his driving mirror. 'I just took it you were talking to Luca.'

She gazed at him crossly. 'How do you know I wasn't telling you what a ridiculous escape plan you had?'

'That's easy,' he said smoothly. 'When you mentioned my name, you smiled.'

This time she saw the glint in his eye and bit back the sharp retort she was going to make. 'You never take anything seriously, do you?' she asked.

He shrugged. 'Yes, I do. World peace, human rights, saving the whale—'

'You know what I mean,' she interrupted.

He looked thoughtfully at the road ahead. 'Oh,' he said softly. 'You mean humdrum things, like being chased by Luca?'

Cara glared at him, but he seemed absolutely impervious. One day, she promised herself suddenly, she would find a chink in this man's armour and find out what really made him tick.

How could he be so flippant when he was under such strain? 'Let me drive,' she offered suddenly. 'I'm perfectly capable, really, and you look as though you could do with a rest.'

He rubbed a hand wearily over his forehead and pulled to the hard shoulder. 'Go on then,' he said simply, getting out of the car so they could swap seats. 'Drive. I like to live dangerously once in a while. Follow the signs for Monte Carlo and Nice and wake me if anything, but anything, looks out of the ordinary.'

The feel of doing something helped release some of the pent-up tension in Cara's body. And as she began to thread tentatively at first, then more confidently in and out of the fast traffic, she began to smile. Finn had been right. At this precise moment, whatever Luca was up to, she was free.

She had been afraid yesterday morning when she had thought of her impending new life, but never in her wildest dreams had she envisaged quite how new it would be. And she wasn't married to Luca. Her smile widening, she glanced at Finn. He was fast asleep.

It was several hours before Cara knew for certain that something was wrong with the car. 'Finn,' she said tentatively. 'Wake up.'

He opened one eye. 'Have we crashed and gone to heaven?'

'We haven't crashed,' she said carefully. 'But the car...
I don't like the sound of it.'

'What?' He was fully alert now, concentrating on the
ominous clattering the engine was making.

'I can't seem to get any power,' she said wretchedly.
'And when I put my foot on the accelerator it just gets
worse.' The car was coasting to a halt on the hard
shoulder, steam billowing from under the bonnet, and
it stopped with a very final-sounding bang.

'That's torn it,' he remarked.

She glared at him. 'You don't seem particularly
heartbroken.'

He shrugged. 'It's a hire car. What's done is done.'

'The question is, what exactly is done? Have we got
a flat tyre or something?'

He stared at her in amazement. 'A flat tyre? Are you
joking?' He leaned across and peered at her face. 'No,'
he said, pulling back. 'You're not joking.'

'I heard this hissing noise,' she said. 'I thought it was
air coming out of the tyre.'

She could see him suppressing a smile and she felt like
banging the steering wheel in frustration. 'Stop making
fun of me!' she yelled. 'Can you make this heap go, or
not?'

'Cara,' he said gently. 'Did you think to look at the
temperature gauge, at all?'

She stared at him uncomprehendingly and then at the
dashboard. 'It's... it's a bit high,' she said in a small
voice.

'It's off the dial,' remarked Finn. 'The engine has
seized, because all the water has fallen out of it. One of
the hoses has probably gone, and that final bang you
heard was the head gasket giving up the ghost.'

'Aren't you even going to look at the engine?' she demanded.

'What for?' he asked.

She pursed her lips and raised her hands to heaven. 'To make sure you're right,' she snapped.

He looked at her carefully. 'Do you know anything about engines?' he asked.

'Of course I don't,' she retorted.

'Uh-huh,' he replied. 'Well, what are you going to do when you've looked at the engine?'

'I'm not going to do anything,' she said blankly. 'I was hoping you could fix it.'

He gave her another look she couldn't quite fathom and then got out of the car. She released the bonnet catch and followed him.

Even Cara could see that the engine was irreparable. 'I suppose you think it was my fault,' she muttered. 'For not looking at that stupid dial.'

He shrugged. 'Damn little we could have done about it, even if you had. It's not as though we have any spare water.'

She lifted her hands helplessly. 'What are we going to do now?'

He smiled. 'Hitch a lift, of course.'

'All the way to England?' she said, amazed.

He pulled the grip out of the boot and locked all the doors. 'Monte Carlo will do for starters,' he replied.

The day was blindingly hot, the sun beating down on the top of their heads and glaring cruelly off the stream of cars rushing past.

The dust and exhaust fumes made Cara want to cough almost constantly, and she felt almost too exhausted to follow Finn any farther.

'It's not far now,' he said, turning and stopping to wait for her. He must be tired, too, she thought, but he wasn't showing it, unless it was in the grim set of his face.

He reached out a hand to her, and speechlessly, she took it. 'You're doing fine,' he encouraged, 'Only a few more yards to the slip road, and we'll be able to thumb a lift easily.'

She knew that he wanted her to respond, to show that she wasn't yet giving in to her exhaustion, and grimly, she nodded.

He squeezed her fingers, and instinctively she squeezed back, feeling a little more cheerful as she followed him down the slip road. 'Here will do nicely,' he said, putting the grip on a grassy verge and looking keenly at the traffic.

'What happens if some of Luca's men stop?' she asked, and then before he could say anything, she shook her head. 'Don't answer that,' she said dully. 'The picture I can see in my mind is terrible enough.'

'That's what I like about you,' remarked Finn. 'You always look on the bright side.'

'I'm a realist,' she said.

'Hmm,' he said. 'Well, here's some realism for you— all the cars going past us now are just joining the autoroute from different towns in France. If we stick to a car with a French number plate, we should be okay.'

At that moment a very old, very decrepit little truck clanked to a stop beside them. After a brief discussion with the driver Finn opened the door and bowed to Cara. 'Your car, madame.'

Cara's jaw dropped. 'That's not a car,' she whispered. 'That's . . . that's—'

'Transport,' said Finn firmly. 'Now get in. Or do you want to travel with the tomatoes in the back?'

Cara got in and nodded tentatively at the driver, an unshaven Frenchman with a cigarette seemingly glued permanently to his lower lip.

Finn heaved himself up beside her, and suddenly there was no space at all in the tiny cab.

'Stop wriggling,' murmured Finn. 'The driver will think you've got fleas.'

She glared at him. 'He'll probably be pleased for the extra company,' she retorted.

He put his arm around her and drew her close. 'That better?' he asked.

His hand was resting on her upper arm, light but sure on her skin, her body cradled against his chest. All she had to do was drop her head on his shoulder and she could sleep forever. But his presence was unsettling. Going to sleep with him holding her would be too intimate, too trusting.

'Go to sleep, Cara,' he said softly.

'I can't,' she replied jerkily.

His free hand came up and slid around her throat, then moved down, settling her more securely against his body. For one split second she stiffened, then as she glanced into his eyes the temptation to do as he said was overwhelming.

Tentatively she lay her head on his shoulder, her senses reeling at his clean, warm male smell, her body revelling unconsciously in the realisation of how much comfort this man could give her.

But how much did all this mean to him? He was a stranger, for all his comforting ways, and she couldn't afford to really trust him. He ought to know that, in case . . . in case he got the wrong idea.

She lifted her head and stared at his face, only inches from her own. 'I don't want to...' She paused and swallowed. Why, all of a sudden, did she feel so nervous? 'I don't want to give you the wrong...impression,' she went on in a rush. 'It was a mistake to let you kiss me yesterday. It didn't mean anything to me, as I'm sure it didn't to you.' She stopped and bit her lip, her heart beating so loudly at the memory, she was sure he could hear it.

'So if you don't want to hold me, that's all right with me,' she added untruthfully. 'I'm only doing this because it seems the most sensible thing to do. This is all just purely a business arrangement. Nothing more. So you needn't think I'm attracted to you at all.'

Cara kept her head up, waiting for his reaction. She'd made her feelings plain, but she couldn't help feeling again how stilted and silly her words seemed. It wasn't until she said them that she realised how much she was beginning to rely on Finn. She waited tensely for him to push her away.

Instead, his arm tightened about her, and his voice when it came seemed oddly amused. 'Of course,' he replied.

'Is that it?' she demanded blankly. It was not the response she had expected at all. Luca, in his position, would have been insulted and angry.

'Cara,' he said softly.

Her heart seemed to do a double somersault. 'Yes?'

He smiled at her. 'Go to sleep.'

She put her head on his shoulder. It was all too much of a puzzle to work out, and she was so tired. But it was nice that Finn hadn't pushed her away. It was very comforting, being held by him.

She didn't realise she had dozed off until the truck stopped and she opened her eyes to find Finn opening the door of the cab.

'Where are we?' she muttered sleepily, stretching languorously against him. Then in an instant she was awake and, reddening slightly, she pulled away from him and sat up straight.

'We're in Monte Carlo,' replied Finn, the amusement at her embarrassment only too evident in his voice. Glaring at him, and stumbling out incoherent thanks to the truck driver, she followed Finn from the cab.

It was only a few minutes' walk into the main square, but with every step of the way Cara became more depressed. She looked around at the sunny streets and the beautifully dressed people strolling past the fountains and the statues that seemed to be everywhere, and pulled self-consciously at her rather grubby shorts.

'After this trip,' she said mutinously to Finn, 'I'm never going anywhere, ever, with you again.'

He hefted the grip in his right hand and took her elbow with the other. 'And I thought you were enjoying it so much,' he said blandly. 'All this adventure after such a sheltered life. It has to be good for you.'

'Look at me,' she demanded, and then as Finn's eyes raked over her body she dropped her eyes and turned away. 'Stop it,' she muttered.

'It was your suggestion,' he said lazily.

'I didn't mean like that,' she said awkwardly, her heart beating unnaturally fast at the message she had read in his gaze. She forced herself to look at him. 'I meant,' she said deliberately, 'that I'm tired and dirty and wearing clothes you wouldn't give a beggar.'

'Thank you,' murmured Finn. 'They're my clothes. And I was quite fond of them.'

She picked morosely at a loose thread in the seam of the shorts. 'Everybody's so beautifully dressed here,' she said at last. 'And everything's so clean and shiny. Even the flowers look like they've been polished.' She swallowed, waves of despondency threatening to envelop her. 'And I'm...'

'Not?' supplied Finn.

She stared at him, not knowing whether to burst into tears or stamp her foot. 'I've been whisked away from the only life I've ever known,' she told him. 'I've been chased and shot at by the man I was supposed to marry, and made fun of by a lunatic with a chocolate gun.'

Finn's lips were twisting, but she rushed on. 'I'm sorry if it was my fault the car broke down, and I'm sorry if you didn't think I was very grateful about being squashed into a tomato lorry, but I—'

She lifted her hands helplessly, then dropped them. Finn put a forefinger under her chin and tipped her face up to his. 'Cara,' he said softly.

She swallowed hard. 'Yes?'

'What would you like most in the world, right now?'

She looked into his eyes, but there was no trace of mockery in them. 'Truly?' she forced out.

'Truly.'

She bit her lip and then said in a small voice, 'A bath. And then a long, proper sleep in a very big bed. And something to eat when I wake up.'

She could see he was smiling at her and she closed her eyes. 'I know it's childish of me,' she said miserably. 'But it's just a daydream, isn't it? You're going to tell me you have to do something about the car and then we'll have to be on the run again.' She looked at her feet. 'I'm trying not to complain, honestly. I know you're doing your best and I really do appreciate everything you've done for me.'

There was silence, and she wondered what he was thinking. Slowly her eyes lifted to his. Finn was putting the grip on the pavement. 'What…what are you doing?' she asked.

'I'm going to kiss you,' he said. 'You are so beautifully practical, Cara, I have to make quite sure you're real.'

'You're making fun of me,' she stammered as his arms slid around her and pulled her close.

'Certainly not,' he said softly. 'I've just never met a woman before whose first priority in Monte Carlo is finding a bath and then a bed.' He smiled at her. 'A woman almost after my own heart.'

'You're twisting my words,' she retorted, her mind filling with all sorts of unsettling images, her heart hammering at his touch.

'Who says?' he demanded softly, and before she could reply he had bent his head to hers, his lips plundering the sweet moisture of her mouth.

Her fists beat against his chest, then, relaxing, slid around his neck. This wasn't right at all. How could she feel this way about a man she had known for less than twenty-four hours? But it was difficult to hang on to any doubts when a man like Finn had his arms about her. Difficult to think coherently at all.

Impossible to think of anything but the texture of his skin, the soft pressure of his lips, the feel of his hair at the nape of his neck. Hungrily she returned his kiss, wanting him with a vehemence that almost terrified her.

'Hush,' he soothed at last, his cool fingers trailing down her hot cheek. 'Let's go find that bath.'

She had a sudden vivid picture of what it would be like to share a bath with Finn—soap bubbles shining on his water-sleek muscles, skin against skin in the warm intimacy of the gently steaming water. She shook her head distractedly. How could she feel this way for him only a day after she had come so close to promising her life to another man?

Her fingers enclosed his hand and drew it away from her face. 'Don't ever do that again,' she said, vaguely conscious as she spoke that passers-by were smiling at them. Smiling at the perfect illusion of a lover's tiff.

'And why not?' Finn drawled, his eyes raking hers.

'Because I don't want you to,' she stammered, the colour rising in her cheeks.

'That's not what your body was telling me a few moments ago,' he pointed out.

'My body's got nothing to do with you!' she flared. 'Leave me alone!'

Another searching look, then a small smile and a shrug. 'All right,' he said and, picking up the grip, sauntered off. Staring after him with mingled anger and frustration, she swore horribly under her breath, then ran to catch him up.

The hotel was a haven of air-conditioning and marble floors and hushed voices. Cara leant against a pillar and watched warily as Finn came away from the desk, the bellboy waiting behind with a key in his hand.

'Don't tell me,' she said icily. She had conjured up a mental picture of what he had arranged, and with every detail she added to it, she became angrier and angrier. She clenched her fists and looked at him. 'You're going to explain you could only get a double room. And how, oh, so unfortunately, it hasn't got separate beds. Aren't you?'

His eyes, if anything, looked even more amused at her tone, but his face remained absolutely impassive. 'I tried to get separate hotels,' he said. 'But no one would have you.'

'What do you mean?' she gasped.

He smiled outright at that, and she could have kicked herself for falling into his trap. 'Well,' he began. 'It was the clothes, mostly, that put them off. And then, of course, there's the fact that you're none too clean, and they do like their guests to have a bit of polish—'

'You beast!' she spluttered.

'See what I mean?' he observed to no one in particular. 'No manners. The things I've had to put up with on this trip. It made their hair curl at the desk, you know—'

'The things *you've* had to put up with?' she asked, following him to the lift and, after its short journey, to the door the bellboy was opening. 'What about me? What about the lunatic things you've got up to?'

Finn pressed a note in to the boy's hand and walked into the room.

'It's a double suite,' murmured Cara, looking around in amazement.

Finn switched off the air-conditioning and opened a tall window looking out on the sea. 'What did you expect?' he said, walking right up to her. 'That I would trick you into sharing my bed?'

His tone was light, but his eyes were hard, and Cara swallowed. 'I didn't know what to think,' she said at last. 'When you kissed me, I—'

'When I kissed you,' he interrupted, 'you enjoyed it. And then you felt guilty. Probably because of some twisted reasoning about Luca. Elementary, my dear Watson.'

'I do not feel guilty!' she snapped.

'No?' he drawled.

There was a look in his eye that made her want to kick him. How dare he be so sure about her? How dare he be so bloody arrogant? She would show him.

'Do you want to make love to me?' she demanded, her head pounding. She stalked up to him with a bravado she didn't feel at all. 'I don't mind. It's no big deal to me. We can do it right here, if you like, on the Chinese rug. Or what about on the sofa?' She patted the soft striped cushions theatrically. 'Nice and firm.' She steeled herself to stare him straight in the eye, but didn't quite make it.

'Or maybe,' she swept on, trying hard to keep up her airy tone, 'maybe you're the kind of man who wants to do it on top of the wardrobe. Let's do it there. I'll just get a chair.'

'Cara.' He caught her hand and pulled her to him.

'Don't touch me!' she burst out, her nerves jerking at his closeness, unable to keep up the facade any longer.

'I can't make love to you if I can't touch you,' he said softly.

'I don't want you to make love to me,' she snapped, her pulse thudding as she tried to struggle away from him. 'I'm just fed up with you having all the answers all the time.'

'Cara!' He gave her a little shake, and she stilled. 'Will you stop behaving like a child?'

She opened her mouth to make some snappy answer and then, as she looked into his eyes, closed it again.

He smiled fleetingly. 'That's better,' he said softly. 'Now go and get some sleep.'

'Do you always order people about like this?' she asked.

'Didn't you know?' he asked huskily. 'My middle name is Napoleon.'

'That figures,' she replied scathingly. But there was nothing else she could say. She *was* tired, and denying it would just be silly. She bit her lip, and with her head held high made for one of the bedrooms and closed the door behind her. She did not once glance back at Finn, but she had the oddest impression he was smiling. Damn him.

It was dark when she woke up, and she could hear a voice in the next room. She lay listening to the indistinct words for a few moments, enjoying the feel of the linen sheets on her sleep-warm skin. No more cramp. Nothing that made her feel as though she had grit in her eyelids and a permanent yawn stitched to her face.

The shower she had had before sleeping had been wonderful. She had been too tired to have a bath, after all. But maybe she would get up and have one before facing Finn once more. She hadn't thanked him, and she probably needed to apologise again, as well.

She sighed as she thought of her outrageous behaviour earlier, then began to wonder who Finn was talking to. Not himself, that was for sure. Because for all her earlier suspicions, he was a long way from being crazy.

Then, as clearly as if she had been in the same room, she heard him say her name. Her heart stilling, she slid from the bed and slipped to the door.

Pushing it open fractionally, she could see Finn on the telephone, pacing up and down the carpet, the receiver clamped to his ear, nodding impatiently at whatever was being said. 'Of course not,' he replied at last. 'What do you take me for? I told you, she suspects nothing.' There was silence, then, 'No, I won't risk it. Yes. Soon. Okay.' The conversation was obviously at an end, and Finn put the receiver down with a clatter and sighed deeply.

Cara watched him move to the window. He fiddled abstractedly with the catch, his mind obviously far away, and she stole back to bed.

Finn's words seemed to hang in the air above her. What had he meant, 'She suspects nothing'?

Cara punched her pillow irritably. Who was he talking to? He'd obviously been talking about her. Had she jumped from the frying pan, slap bang into the fire? She pulled the blankets almost over her head and thought of the way Finn had seen off Luca at the service station. He couldn't be out to deceive her. He couldn't. Could he?

Her heart was pounding, and her palms were damp. If Finn was out to betray her, then she was truly on her own. And she wouldn't give much odds for her survival. There was no way she could escape from her family and from him. What was he up to?

A sudden rattling at the door almost stopped her breathing, and then with an effort she closed her eyes. Whatever happened she mustn't let Finn know she had overheard him. It was a tiny advantage, but it was the only one she had.

She could hear his quiet, almost catlike tread as he came up to the bed, then the creak and shift of the mattress as he sat beside her.

'Come on, Cara,' he said. 'Time to get up.'

She kept her eyes closed, then as his fingers pulled the sheets from her face and trailed lightly over her cheek, her body almost jolted with the shock.

'I can tell by your breathing that you're wide awake,' he remarked. 'So there's no point in pretending you're asleep.'

'Yes, there is,' she muttered indistinctly. 'You might go away then.'

'I might get in beside you,' he drawled.

She jerked bolt upright, holding the sheet to her body. 'You wouldn't dare!'

His eyes were only inches from her own, and full of amusement. 'Why not?' he murmured. 'It looks a very warm and comfortable place to be.'

'My feet get very cold,' she said in a rush. 'You wouldn't like it.'

He leant across and kissed her full on the lips. 'On the contrary,' he murmured. 'It sounds wonderful. And I, for one, never get cold feet.'

With a gasp, she pulled the sheet more closely around her and wriggled out of bed, tugging at the fine linen to free it from the blankets, then backed away from him across the thick pale green carpet. 'You wouldn't dare!'

He smiled at her, then plumped up the pillows and stretched out full length on the bed.

'What... what are you doing?' she asked uncertainly.

He clasped his hands and put them behind his head. 'Waiting for you to get dressed, of course,' he said smoothly.

How dare he look so comfortable on her bed! Her pulse began to rattle uncontrollably at the sight of his body sprawled so easily where she had been lying only seconds before.

'Why don't you go and lie on your own bed?' she snapped, pulling a corner of the sheet more tightly round herself and tucking it in over the top. It was so tight now, she was having difficulty breathing.

'Tell me something,' he remarked, smiling at her.

'What?' she asked suspiciously.

'Are you rehearsing for a part in *The Return of the Mummy*?' he inquired. 'Because if you are, I may as well tell you now that some of your wrappings are coming adrift.'

'What?' she squeaked, realising from a sudden airy feeling behind her that the other corner of the sheet had dropped completely and that she would be completely exposed if she turned around.

Fury began hissing through her veins. How could he make fun of her like this? How could he? Without even thinking, she reached for the bedside light and grabbed it, yanking its flex from the socket. 'Do you know what you are?' she yelled, throwing it at him. 'Do you really know what you are?'

Finn caught the light easily and sat up, looking speculatively at her.

'Don't you come near me,' she screamed, suddenly nervous at the glint in his eye. 'I'll kill you!'

'What with?' he asked.

She caught up an ornament on the table and threw that at him, as well. But it landed harmlessly in the bed where he had been, because he had got up and was standing in front of her, holding her hands and pulling her to him, the sheet dragging from her body.

'Let me go,' she said breathlessly.

'Listen to me, Cara,' he said quietly. 'We haven't got a great deal of time.' Shocked by the evenness of his tone, she fell silent.

'You have to get up and get dressed,' he went on. 'Luca is on his way here.'

'What?' she gasped.

His hand cupped her cheek briefly. 'It's all right,' he said quietly. 'We've got several hours' head start, but we have to get out of here. It's just unfortunate that we haven't got time for a row, much as I enjoy a good dramatic one.'

Her heart pounding, she stared at him, letting the lightness of his words wash over her, reading the truth in his eyes. She nodded slowly, her anger seeping away, her mind full of the implications of what he had just said.

'Cara,' he said softly, as she stepped away. She turned questioningly.

'Haven't you forgotten something?' he asked, holding up the sheet.

Her heart lurched. 'Give it to me,' she snapped, her stomach clenching with the realisation that she was completely naked in front of him.

Without a word he pressed it into her hands.

'And you can stop smiling like that,' she burst out, hurriedly wrapping it around herself. 'It's not funny.'

He looked at her with an expression that made her heart beat even faster. 'I wasn't laughing at you,' he said quietly. There was a seriousness in his tone that made her catch her breath, then she ran for the shelter of the bathroom, knowing in her heart that she was running not from Finn, but from her own ridiculous desires.

'Cara,' he said once more, and her hand stilled on the door handle.

She turned uncertainly, and after a fractional pause he shook his head. 'It doesn't matter,' he replied at last.

CHAPTER FIVE

CARA glared at him, feeling somehow that she had missed something and angry at the way he was affecting her. 'Do you know what you are?' she demanded again.

'Yes.' He yawned, sitting on the bed. 'People tell me all the time.' He pointed through the doorway. 'I did some shopping for you while you were asleep.'

She glanced at the bags heaped on the sitting room carpet. 'You bought clothes for me?' she said blankly, hitching the sheet more tightly around her. 'How do you know I'll like them? Or that they'll fit?'

He shrugged. 'Only one way to tell. Of course,' he added, 'you can always wear my shorts again, if you prefer.'

'But—'

'No buts,' he interrupted, looking at his watch. 'We have to be on our way again soon, and if you want something to eat as well, you better hurry.'

The clothes fitted perfectly when she tried them on in her bathroom, and Cara squashed down the thoughts about how Finn must have sized her up. Not that there was anything very startling in what he had bought, mostly practical shirts and shorts and a couple of cotton dresses. She held one of them at arm's length. It was well cut and pretty. He had a good eye, that much was certain.

She thought again of how he had looked at her, and dressed hurriedly.

Cara felt strangely self-conscious when she entered the bedroom. Finn was still lying on the bed, staring at the ceiling as if he was trying to work out long division in his head.

He looked at her, though, as soon as she came through the door. 'Everything fit okay?'

'Yes, thanks,' she said as lightly as she could.

He nodded. 'The girl in the shop put in a box of underclothes, too,' he said.

'I got them,' she replied. She felt awkward and uncertain of what to say next. 'Must have been quite a sight,' she joked at last. 'You in a dress shop.'

He rubbed his chin thoughtfully. 'It was an experience,' he admitted. 'But I still can't understand why women take so long shopping. I was in and out in half an hour.'

She shrugged. 'That's because you don't have to wear the clothes you bought. It's a very psychological thing.'

He nodded slowly. 'That's what every woman I've ever known has told me,' he said. 'And I've never believed any of them.'

Cara turned and picked up a hairbrush with studied casualness. 'You make it sound as though you've had this conversation a hundred times before,' she remarked.

She could hear the mattress squeaking as he got up, and her hand stilled momentarily as his face appeared behind hers in the mirror. She swallowed and kept brushing, trying not to meet his eye. 'I've got ninety-nine sisters,' he said softly.

His breath was warm on her cheek, and smelled faintly of toothpaste. As she stared in the mirror she noticed as if for the first time his long-lashed eyes, strong nose and wide, sensual mouth. He smelled of soap and clean clothes, and she breathed deep, as if to steady herself, but seeing instead her hands begin to shake more uncontrollably.

His hand strayed onto hers as she put the brush down and she twisted round to face him, her heart thundering at the message in his eyes. 'This isn't right, Finn,' she said unsteadily. His face was only inches from hers.

'It doesn't matter whether it's right or not,' he said huskily. 'It's how we both feel.'

It would be so easy to give in to her instincts, to reach up and stroke his cheek, to kiss him on those full, wide lips. But then Cara thought of the phone call she had overheard earlier and she pushed away from him. 'It's not how I feel,' she said stiffly. 'I don't feel anything.'

He twined a strand of her hair around his fingers. 'Liar,' he replied.

'Let me go,' she demanded.

'I'm not touching you,' he said gently.

And it was true. His hands had dropped to his sides. She saw the mocking look in his eyes and she spun round to the mirror, furiously beginning to brush her hair once more. But he didn't go away.

'Haven't you got anything more interesting to do than just stand there and stare at me?' she snapped.

'I like looking at what you're thinking,' he said easily.

'And just what do you mean by that?' she demanded, trying and failing to steady her voice.

'Well,' he began, crossing his arms. 'The way you look when you're angry, for example. You get these two little creases between your eyebrows and your eyes start sparking like an overloaded welding kit.'

Her hand holding the hairbrush stilled.

'And then, of course,' he continued, 'there's that I don't care if you drop dead look—you know, the one when you lift your chin and absolutely dare me to disagree with you.'

Cara turned, her hand raised, holding the hairbrush. Finn stared at her. 'You going to hit me with that, or give me a new hairstyle?' His hand caught hers easily, and for a moment they stood staring at each other.

'I am not attracted to you in any way, shape or form,' she said stiffly. 'It's just your enormous ego that makes you think I want to climb into bed with you.'

He stared at her for a long moment, then he began to smile at her.

'What's wrong?' she asked. 'Can't take the truth? Think I'm joking?'

'Oh, Cara,' he said gently, dropping her hand. 'You are the most extraordinary woman.'

'I am not,' she snapped.

His lips twitched. 'You are the one who keeps talking about going to bed with me,' he murmured. 'I'm sure I've never mentioned it.'

Her jaw dropped. 'You practically climbed in with me, not half an hour ago!' she argued, realising too late that he was winding her up once more.

'Did I?' he asked innocently. 'How terribly careless of me.'

'And you kissed me!' she accused. 'Several times.'

'And of course,' he drawled, 'one just naturally follows on from the other.'

Her heart lurched. His face was expressionless except perhaps for a little glint of amusement in those too blue eyes. Perhaps she had misread him. Perhaps he really had affected her more than she affected him. She compressed her lips. Damn his arrogance. 'You know what I mean,' she said crossly. 'The way you—'

'The way I what?' he interrupted.

She gritted her teeth. 'The way you are!' she burst out.

He shrugged. 'Well, there's not much I can do about that,' he said. 'Or about the fact that I quite like kissing you, and I know you like it, too.'

'You arrogant—' she breathed. 'You don't know anything about me! And you are not to kiss me any more. Do you hear?'

He smiled outright as he gave her a mock salute. 'Yes, ma'am,' he snapped, then looked at her thoughtfully. 'Or is it no, ma'am?' He drew her towards him. 'You see,' he said softly, kissing her once more. 'I always forget which way round it goes.'

Angrily she struggled against him, then realised that he had let her go.

'I meant it,' she gasped, sitting on the edge of the bed. 'I don't want you to touch me.'

'Because of Luca?' he drawled.

'Of course not,' she snapped. Too quickly. 'What has Luca got to do with anything?'

He sat beside her. 'Nothing much, I guess,' he replied. 'Except that if circumstances were different this would be Luca and not me sitting next to you. Luca . . . your husband.'

'Well, he's not my husband!' she shouted.

'But you still miss him, don't you?' he said calmly. 'After all, he's been part of your life for so long, it can't have been easy to leave him like that.'

Cara glared at him, tears standing in her eyes. 'I miss my family, not Luca,' she admitted.

Finn looked at her curiously. 'He and your uncle were practically the only close family you had, weren't they? Luca's known you since you were a child. And I remember reading how your uncle took Luca under his

wing when Luca's father died. Practically brought him
up as his own son, despite all the accusations from the
rest of the Finzi family that he was just doing it for Luca's
inheritance.'

She clenched her hands. 'I forgot you knew so much
about my life,' she said coldly. 'What is this? An interview for your book? What do you want to know
about—my second cousin's ice-cream factory? Maybe
my other cousin's olive-oil business would get you going.
Or are you just interested in digging whatever dirt you
can find or make up?'

'Of course,' he drawled, his voice dangerously light.
'I've got the tape recorder running now.'

She knew she had gone too far. Knew that he was
angry with her. He had tried to be kind, and she had
bitten his head off. She could tell without even looking
at him. Nervously she got up and stood with her back
to him. 'I've gone off the deep end again,' she said stiffly.
'And I'm sorry. Again. Truly, I am. But I just can't get
over what has happened. That I've deserted my family.'

He reached for her hand and pulled her gently round
to face him. 'Is that how you feel?' he asked. 'A
deserter?'

She stared at him, unable to put any of her swirling
emotions into words.

He shook his head. 'You shouldn't feel that way. Luca
needed deserting. Preferably in the Sahara. And up to
his neck in sand.

'But as for the rest of your family, I don't know.' He
shrugged. 'You were in an impossible situation. If your
uncle loves you, he'll realise that. He'll come round in
the end. And so will all your second and third cousins.
As far as I can tell, no one has much love for your erst-
while bridegroom.'

'In my family some things are more important than love,' Cara said bitterly. 'Like duty and honour and all that stuff. Uncle Pancrazio told me once he gave up the greatest love of his life because the honour of his family came first.'

'And he expected you to marry Luca for the same reason?' probed Finn grimly.

She nodded slowly, a little frightened of the black look on his face.

His next question took her completely by surprise. 'How old are you?' he demanded.

'Twenty-one,' she replied, taken aback. 'It was my birthday yesterday.'

He said something unprintable under his breath, then got up and stalked to the window.

She bit her lip and looked at the carpet. 'Are you sorry you rescued me?' she asked in a low voice. Stupid question. Luca was after him, too, now. And there would be no escape. Of course he had to regret helping her.

He swung round to look at her and suddenly she didn't want him to answer her, just in case she was right.

She swallowed the lump in her throat. 'Maybe I haven't escaped far enough.' She forced the words out, attempting a joke. 'Maybe I should run away to a nunnery, somewhere off the beaten track, like Mars.'

He crossed the room in two short strides and squatted in front of her. There were tears glittering on her eyelashes, and he brushed them away with his thumb, his fingers cupping her cheek. 'Now that really would be a shame,' he said softly, trying hard to make her smile. 'Because I was quite looking forward to that session on top of the wardrobe.'

She drew a raggedy breath and opened her mouth to say something, but was drowned out by a sudden loud knocking on the door.

'Luca,' she breathed, her heart stilling.

'I doubt it,' replied Finn drily, getting to his feet. 'But stay here, all the same.'

She followed him to her door and kept it open a crack as he crossed the sitting room. He spoke a few low words before opening the main door. Nodding slightly, as if at a reply, he turned the knob.

It was not Luca on the threshold. In fact, it was no one she recognised. But the man and woman who walked into the room looked vaguely familiar. She couldn't think where she'd seen them before.

She came out at Finn's call and smiled uncertainly at the pair, remembering only too vividly the overheard phone call and wondering what was in store for her now.

'Who are they?' she breathed.

'Police,' said Finn, matter-of-factly. 'They're going to take our places.'

He shot a glance at her, then continued, 'They want to catch Luca almost as much as he wants to catch us, and this is the perfect bait.'

'But what about England? Sarah? My plan?'

'It's on hold for a while, that's all,' he replied. 'If you think about it, as long as Luca is on the loose, you'll never be able to escape. You have to help catch him.'

Her whole body sagged as the enormity of what he was saying sank in. She sat down. 'I can't,' she whispered.

Finn stared at her, his face expressionless. 'Do you still love him?' he demanded.

'No,' she said, stung. 'I never did. I told you.'

He sat beside her and turned her face to his. 'What then?' he asked.

She swallowed hard. 'It's like you said,' she told him at last. 'Luca is part of my family. Yesterday I came within seconds of becoming his wife. Last night would have been our wedding night.'

She trailed off and breathed deeply to try to stop the way her body was trembling. 'I'm glad I ran away,' she said at last. 'I'm glad. And I'd like nothing better than for Luca to stop chasing me. But I don't want to trap him.'

'You think he's just going to give up and go home?' demanded Finn.

'Eventually, maybe,' she lied as stoutly as she could.

Finn stood and paced to and fro. 'Eventually?' he said, his voice loaded with disbelief. 'Well, eventually the world will come to an end and we can all stop worrying. But that day won't be tomorrow.'

'You're exaggerating,' she countered, twisting her fingers together. 'And in any case—' she glanced up at Finn, his outline black against the sunshine flooding through the window ' —Luca's got a mistress. He'll have to go back to her sometime and forget about me.'

Finn pulled her to her feet and shook her. 'Forget about you?' he raged. 'The only way he'll forget about you and the massive dent you've put in his pride is when he's got rid of you permanently! Why can't you see that?'

'Because I'm frightened!' she shouted at him. 'Don't you understand? I don't want to think about him! I hate him and I'm scared of him and I never want to see him again!'

There was silence. Finn's fingers were biting into her arms, her feet barely touching the floor. And then she did something she would never have dared do with Luca when he was in one of his crazy rages. Not after that first time, anyway. She looked him in the eye.

Finn held her gaze and then, his grip loosening, let her down to stand on her own two feet once more. 'You are the most irritating woman I've ever met,' he said at last. 'Crazy, wrong-headed...' Absent-mindedly he rubbed her arms where he had gripped them. 'You okay?' he asked.

'Yes,' she whispered.

'Look,' he said. 'I'm sorry I flew off the handle, but the idea of just leaving Luca to swan about Europe searching for you is so off the wall I couldn't believe my ears.'

'Did you plan this idea of a trap with the police while I was asleep?' she demanded.

He nodded.

She crossed her arms and stalked to the sofa. 'You didn't even ask me!' she raged. 'You treat me just like Luca did. Decide what you think is best for me and then maybe tell me later or not at all.'

Finn took a step towards her. 'Now just wait one second—'

'I'm free,' she flung at him. 'I can do what I like. I don't need to take orders any more.'

Finn gazed at her for a long moment and then nodded grimly. 'Fine. Okay. If that's how you want it.'

She glanced uncertainly at him. He pointed to the door. 'There's the exit,' he said calmly. 'Nice knowing you. What kind of flowers would you like at your funeral? Lilies?'

She stood looking at him, her chin up, then stalked to the door. But Finn's hand was over hers as she reached for the handle. 'Don't be so stupid,' he said roughly, pulling her to him. 'Just how far do you think you're going to get?'

'I don't care,' she spat, struggling against him. 'But I'll get there on my own.'

She kicked out, but he covered his body with hers, backing her against the door, stifling her attempts to hit him. His hand was cupping the side of her face, and she tried to duck away from it. 'Don't,' he ordered.

'Why?' she demanded, attempting to lash out again. He leant more heavily against her. 'Because if I move my hand you'll do yourself serious injury on the hat peg.'

Her body stilled, and she eyed him warily. 'Attagirl,' he said softly. And then he bent his head and kissed her. She didn't want to respond. She didn't want to show that she cared anything for him at all.

But she couldn't help the catch in her heart when he looked at her like that, the feeling of utter wantonness when his fingers strayed down her neck, warmth flooding her skin, and all the time kissing her as though he wanted to possess her utterly.

There was a movement behind them, and Finn pulled away. One of the police officers, the woman, had come into the room and was looking at them while pretending not to. There was a look on her face as she glanced at Finn and then at Cara that took Cara a few seconds to interpret.

Envy. It was envy, Cara realised with a jolt, and then looked at Finn as he took her hand and led her to the sofa. Of course, he was a very handsome man. But she had never thought of how other women would react to him.

He sat down and tugged her down next to him. 'Well,' he said. 'Maybe we ought to start this conversation again.

I'm sorry I didn't consult you earlier. But you were asleep and I didn't see how you could object.'

She bit her lip. 'I'm sorry, too,' she said at last. 'I just don't like being pushed into a corner and then told what I must do.'

There was a muscle thudding in his jaw. 'Unless it's your family pushing you into a corner and telling you to marry Luca,' he retorted drily.

She shook her head. 'That's not what I meant at all,' she said hotly. 'I'm free now. I don't have to be pushed around any longer. I just want to lead my own life. If I go all out to trap Luca, then that makes me just as bad as him. So why should I?'

He put his fingers under her chin and turned her face towards him. 'Because if you don't,' he said with utter seriousness, 'he will either kill you, or you will stay frightened all your life.'

His fingers dropped, and she stood up and gazed unseeingly out the window. 'What about my uncle?' she asked with an attempt at bravado she didn't feel. 'Do you want me to trap him, too?'

There was silence at that, and she turned to him. His face had a closed look she had never seen before. 'Well?' she demanded.

'Cara,' he said gently, 'I think maybe you better sit down.'

Something was wrong. She could tell from his face. 'What's happened?' she asked. 'Tell me.'

He looked her straight in the eye and sighed. 'It seems that after you left the church, your uncle had an attack.'

'An attack?' she echoed, horrified.

'A heart attack,' he explained.

Suddenly she was finding it difficult to breathe. 'I have to go back,' she whispered.

Finn got up and stood in front of her. 'You can't,' he snapped, and then after a pause added more gently, 'you know you can't.'

She pushed at him with her fists, but he didn't move, merely holding her wrists with his hands, letting her continue to beat against him. 'I have to,' she cried. 'He's been like a father to me. I can't desert him now!'

'Listen to me,' said Finn urgently, transferring both her wrists to one hand and circling her raging body with his other arm.

'Let me go!' she yelled, kicking at him.

He shook her and, startled, she stared at him full face. 'You can't go back,' he told her. 'Think about it.'

She glared at him and lifted her chin. 'Why can't I?'

His grip relaxed slightly, but not enough for her to get away. 'Because you wouldn't get within a hundred miles of him. You ran out on him, remember? And all the rest of your family. And even if you did go back, what then? What could you possibly do? By all accounts it wasn't a very serious attack. He's in the best hospital in Naples, and everything that can be done is being done. From all I hear, he'll be back on his feet in no time.'

Her eyes dropped as she pictured the scene in the church, the white, strained look on her uncle's face when she took Finn's hand. 'It's my fault,' she said dully. 'I should never have run away.'

Finn gave her a little shake. 'Don't be ridiculous.'

She glared at him. 'It's true. I should never have trusted you!'

She could see his jaw tightening, the pupils in his eyes contracting with anger. She waited for him to turn on her, as Luca would have done.

She could feel herself trembling, waiting for the on-slaught, but still he kept looking at her as if he could see right down into the bottom of her heart and was coolly turning over all that he found there.

'And what would you do now,' he pressed, 'if you did manage to see your uncle? Promise to marry Luca?'

She swallowed and looked him straight in the face. 'If necessary,' she replied coldly. 'Yes.'

The temperature in the room seemed to drop by twenty degrees. 'And do you think Luca would have you now?' he asked quietly. 'No matter how much you grovelled to him?'

His words were like a blow in the face, and her head snapped back as if he had hit her. 'I'm beginning to see how brutal you can be, Finn,' she whispered. 'I thought Luca was bad, but he just uses physical violence. You take people apart with your words.'

His eyes had not lifted once from her face. 'I'm not saying this because I want to hurt you,' he said deliberately. 'I'm trying to make you see things clearly for once.'

Her lips parted but he swept on. 'Let's say, in spite of everything, you do manage to go back and marry Luca. What happens then if your uncle dies? In spite of your noble sacrifice? Luca will be able to take over the family business, and your life won't be worth living.' Finn dropped her arms and turned away. 'Think about it, Cara. I'm painting a deliberately bleak picture, I know. But whatever you do now isn't going to affect your uncle's health. And if you go back, you'll be playing right into Luca's hands.'

He shrugged. 'I'll say one thing for your uncle. If he hadn't been taken to hospital, Luca would never have dared shoot at us. You would probably have been back home by now, ironing your wedding dress. But the advantage, if you can call it one, is that with Luca off the leash he is bound to overplay his hand, which means, with any luck, the police will catch him.'

Cara sat numbly on the sofa and rubbed her wrists. Never in her whole life had she felt so alone.

'You're right, I suppose,' she said stiffly at last. 'Although I hate to say it.' She realised she was biting a nail and dropped her hand hurriedly. She was trying very hard to kick the habit. 'I never thought of all this when I left the church with you. I didn't think of anything except that I had to get away.'

She looked at Finn. 'And now I don't know what to do. I am so worried about my uncle I just can't think straight.'

He sat beside her once more and took her hand. 'From all the police tell me,' he said, 'he seems to have a very good chance of recovering. What we have to worry about is Luca. You're right—you don't have to help if you don't want to. But this trap will go ahead, whether you agree or not. The police have provided a safe house for us until it is all over. I think it would be good idea to take them up on their offer.'

She stared at him steadily. 'I have no choice, do I?' she said.

He shook his head wearily. 'No.'

Both the officers were in the room. The man said a few words to Finn, who looked at Cara and then replied in French.

'What are they saying?' she asked irritably.

He turned to her and held out a hand. 'They're saying we better get a move on.'

Cara looked at the couple, checking windows and doors in the sitting room and moving certain pieces of furniture. 'Why do I feel as though I've seen them before,' she asked.

He pulled her to her feet. 'You have,' he said easily. 'In the mirror.'

Her lips parted as light dawned. 'You mean,' she said, 'they're supposed to look like us?'

Finn nodded. 'They're going to make very sure that certain people they suspect of being on Luca's payroll get to hear that we're here. Then, if Luca comes to take the bait, and there's no reason he shouldn't—after all, this is a fairly high-profile place—then they will be able to roll up a good bit of his operation in this part of the world. They're not bad look-alikes,' he added. 'From a distance. Probably better dressed, though,' he mused. 'But then, that's the French for you.'

She glared at him. 'The Italians have much more style than the French,' she retorted, angry at how easy he made it all sound. 'Their fashion houses, for example—'

With a movement of his hand, he stopped her in mid-flow. 'Much as I would like to listen to your dissertation on differing European fashions,' he drawled, 'I really do think we should get a move on. I've been told that, as we thought, Luca wasn't hurt at all in that crash this morning, but I shouldn't think it did much for his temper.'

'How do you know all these things?' she demanded as he hustled her out of the room and down the back stairs of the hotel to where a car was waiting.

Finn put her new carrier bags and his grip in the boot. 'It's my job to know things,' he said. 'Especially when my life is on the line.'

She stared at him uncertainly as he opened the door for her. 'Are you...are you in cahoots with anyone?' she asked at last, his telephone conversation looming large in her mind.

He smiled lazily at her. And she felt her heart beat twice in the space of time he took to reply. 'What a quaint turn of phrase you have,' he said at last, opening the passenger door for her. 'Come on,' he added, motioning to her. 'Get in. We have a long way to go.'

The road, a shimmering pale grey ribbon, wound into the countryside, with the fields of lavender and vineyards on either side seemingly flattened by the hot, pale sky.

Cara was used to the hot Italian summers, but she had always spent the afternoon in the cool of her uncle's villa. Now it was as though she could feel the sun beating down on the roof of the car, the air rushing in through the wide open windows as hot as that in a tumble dryer.

'Are we lost?' she asked tentatively, lifting her hair and holding it on top of her head in a vain attempt to feel a little cooler. 'We seemed to have been going round and round in circles for ages.'

Finn glanced at her and smiled at her makeshift hairstyle. 'Not circles,' he said. 'Zigzags. Blame the road builder. Not me.'

And then he turned off down a track Cara hadn't noticed and drove the protesting car towards a clump of pine trees.

They stopped by a little house, and Finn handed her a bunch of keys. 'Here,' he said. 'Fancy opening up while I put the car away?'

As she took the key-ring their fingers touched, and she was struck suddenly by the normality of his remark. As if they were a married couple, instead of a pair of near strangers one step ahead of disaster.

The house was hot and airless, and Cara's spirits bombed as she took in the smallness of the rooms and cheapness of the furniture. It somehow made her escape seem furtive, as if she was the guilty party, destined always to be on the run. But determinedly she went through the rooms opening the shutters, noting the ornamental bars on the windows and trying not to wonder how good they would be at keeping anyone out.

She stared out through the bars of the sitting room window at the great flat valley stretching away from the house. And she knew without turning round that Finn was behind her. 'This house isn't really you, is it?' he said, taking two large paper carriers to the kitchen.

'I don't know what you mean,' she said quickly, following him to help unpack the food.

He put the bags on the table and eyed her knowingly. 'Yes, you do,' he drawled. 'You're used to a spacious villa with armies of servants and a swimming pool big enough to house the Pacific fleet. This whole house could probably fit quite happily in your uncle's shoe cupboard.'

'I like small houses,' she said defiantly, standing across the table from him. 'It's harder to lose things.'

'People who live in them generally have less things to lose,' he replied.

She put a bag of potatoes on the counter. 'How do you know?' she said truculently. 'Are you one of these people who used to live in a cardboard box in the gutter and who now has to let everybody know how you dragged yourself up by the bootstraps?'

He smiled at her as if at some private joke, and she snorted.

'Do that again,' he said.

'What?' she demanded, off guard once more.

'Snort,' he said simply. 'It's very cute.'

She glared at him. 'Would you like me to kick you?' she snapped.

'Not particularly, no,' he replied, beginning to rummage in the bag nearest him. 'Who's going to do the cooking?'

CHAPTER SIX

CARA stared at him amazed. 'Me, of course.'

'I take it you can cook, then,' Finn said, taking out three peppers and beginning to juggle with them.

'Of course I can,' she retorted. She stared, fascinated in spite of herself, at what he was doing. 'What do you take me for?'

'Well,' he said innocently, 'I mean, you reckoned you could drive....'

This time she saw the glint in his eye before she said anything. 'I'm sorry my driving scared you,' she said sweetly. 'But we Italians lead life in the fast lane, unlike you laid-back American types.'

He kept right on juggling, as if he wasn't really aware of what he was doing, and looked at her interestedly. 'Does that mean you serve dinner at a hundred and twenty miles an hour?'

'I won't serve it at all if you don't give me those peppers,' she said, exasperated.

Without missing a beat he threw the peppers at her one by one, and too surprised to do anything else, she caught them.

He flashed her a smile. 'Guess we'll have to have my speciality cheese on toast tomorrow then,' he said, and went outside.

It was not until later, long after he had eaten and praised the simple meal she had made, that she realised how neatly he had sidestepped the issue of his background. She still knew hardly anything of him. She didn't even know whether she was right to trust him the way she did.

As the evening wore on, the quietness of the house began to get on Cara's nerves. She had gone to bed early, saying she was tired. But that wasn't really true. She had gone to bed early because of Finn. She had never spent so much time on her own with a man before. Not even Luca.

In fact, she realised with a bitter little smile, after Luca had proposed she had spent a great deal of time avoiding him. Then she had made the excuse to herself that it was nerves. Now she knew better. She had just disliked his company.

But Finn. She turned uneasily in her hard little bed and cursed the creaking springs that she was sure he could hear. She didn't want him to think she was awake. Especially not awake and thinking of him.

It was so natural, somehow, to be with him. So easy. And yet at times she found the tension unbearable. The way he had sat so close to her over their meal. The table was so tiny he had had little choice, but all through the meal she had found herself wanting to stare at him, wanting to touch him. And yet she was jolted by the way their knees kept bumping, the way he looked at her when he handed her the salt cellar, his long capable fingers brushing lightly over hers.

She had tried to keep her eyes on her plate, but it had been almost impossible to ignore her instincts. And there had been times when she had looked up to find him staring at her, an expression in his eyes that made her know he wanted her.

There had been none of his easy conversation over the meal, either. He had seemed preoccupied, and she hadn't liked to intrude. Hadn't wanted him to give her any more notice while she was still attempting to sort out her jumbled feelings.

He probably wasn't attracted to her at all, she told herself fiercely. It was probably another one of his wind-ups. After all, he was somewhere in his early thirties and she was only twenty-one—and nearly another man's bride, to boot.

It was so silent here, that was the trouble. They could practically hear each other's hearts beat. Of course, there was the steady thrumming of the cicadas, but that somehow made the silence louder.

The noise of those busy rhythmic insects was like a pulse in her blood, an endless, steady drumbeat that made her want Finn to take her in his arms like he had done that afternoon at the hotel. To draw his beautiful long fingers over her skin. To cancel out every piece of reality except the rising crescendo of the cicadas and the passionate immediacy of here and now.

But of course, nothing had happened. She had cleared the plates with almost indecent haste, washed up and scuttled off to her room. The odd thing about it, though, was that for once Finn, who was normally so acutely observant of the way she was acting, had not even seemed to notice.

Cara sighed and laid the back of her wrist on her forehead. She was imagining things. She was nothing more to Finn than some sort of unwelcome, even dangerous parcel. He was so good-looking he probably tried that easy charm on every girl he met. And since she had rebuffed him, he had got the message and was going to keep his distance.

The trouble was, she remembered only too vividly the way she had felt when he kissed her. And she wanted to feel that way again, she wanted... Cara gritted her teeth.

It was too hot in her room. That was the trouble. Savagely she kicked at the single sheet over her, which had got tangled round her legs, and then with an effort of will not to lose her temper with a piece of cloth, she sat up and pulled the linen straight.

She lay down again as though she was a hospital patient all ready for a bed inspection and closed her eyes. She must go to sleep. She must. But when she closed her eyes it was worse, because then she could see Finn quite clearly, smiling at her, kissing her, covering her body with his as he pushed her against the hotel door.

Damn. She swore horribly under her breath, then sat up and swung her legs to the cool tiled floor. Maybe she should get a glass of water. She pulled the sheet around her, then stopped, remembering only too clearly what had happened in the hotel that afternoon. What if Finn came into the kitchen while she was there? She had better get something more substantial to cover herself with than just a sheet.

A picture of herself driving into the kitchen in a Sherman tank made her giggle suddenly in the quiet room, and hurriedly she stopped. Perhaps she was getting hysterical.

She rummaged quickly in the carriers Finn had given her and found a pair of pyjamas. They were silk, heavy cream silk, and as she slipped them on she wondered who had chosen them, Finn or the sales assistant. Again she thought of how he must have sized her up and how he had looked at her that afternoon when she had scrambled out of bed.

If it had been Finn who had chosen them, though, he had made one outstanding mistake—the legs were about six inches too long. Carefully she turned up the bottoms, and then, straightening, made sure all the buttons on the jacket were fastened.

Nervously she ran her fingers over her head, stroking the long, tight braid she had pulled her hair into. The feel of it snaking through her fingers was oddly comforting.

Finn's bedroom door was closed, she noticed as she slipped from her room, and she tiptoed past it so as not to wake him. She switched on the kitchen light and blinked in its brightness.

Gingerly she got a glass and took a bottle of mineral water from the fridge. And then, her fingers poised, she heard the noise outside quite clearly. She stood perfectly still, her heart jerking, and again there was the sound of footsteps scrunching quietly on the gravel path.

The steps were coming closer, right up to the door. She turned quickly, every sense on the alert. The stainless steel edge of the drainer was pushing into her spine as she gazed at the doorknob slowly turning. With a sudden jolt she realised it wasn't locked. How could Finn have forgotten such a simple thing? Especially when he had closed all the shutters.

Her heart hammering, she noticed that the bolts had not been shot home. And it was too late to do anything about them now—she could never get across the kitchen in time. Please God, please, let it not be Luca.

Without even thinking, she switched off the light. Temporarily blind in the sudden dark, she thought of Finn again. There was no way she could get to him in time. No way to warn him, other than to scream her head off. And that would just alert Luca that they were forewarned. Even so, they couldn't get out. The bars on the windows saw to that.

Her outstretched hand felt and then closed around an unopened bottle of wine on the counter. She hefted it and slid behind the door. Maybe she could still give Finn a chance, after all.

The door was opening. Softly, as if the intruder didn't want to wake anyone. That was certainly Luca's style, thought Cara bitterly. He would want to get right up to their beds before shooting them. Grimly she tightened her grip on the shiny neck of the bottle and lifted it above her head.

If only she hadn't switched the light on in the first place. It was difficult now, after its brightness, to focus on anything clearly.

The intruder was the other side of the door. She could almost feel his presence in the velvet dark. One more step and she would swing down with the bottle. As she tensed for the blow the intruder stepped into the room and closed the door behind him. And he was turning round to her. His hands grabbing for her. She lunged with the bottle, but he was too quick for her, too strong.

And the turn-ups on her pyjama trousers had unravelled, the silk too slippery to hold in one place. Cursing, she tripped, banging helplessly into the stranger. One of his hands snatched the bottle of wine, and she knew with hopeless clarity that she had done everything wrong. But she could still give Finn a chance. Opening her mouth, she began to scream.

In a split second a hand was clamped over her mouth, and she lashed out, kicking and biting. She heard a muttered oath and then a voice she knew only too well. 'Will you be quiet?' Finn whispered, pulling her closer and switching the light on. 'What the hell do you think you're playing at?'

'Me playing at?' she demanded, wrenching her pyjama jacket straight. 'I thought—'

'Don't tell me,' he said grimly, sucking the edge of his hand. 'You thought you were auditioning for grand opera. Either that, or Dracula.'

His eyes raked over her body, and with angry dignity she hitched up her trousers, stumbling a little as she backed away from him. She could feel heat flooding through her skin at the look in his eyes. 'I thought you were Luca,' she snapped, folding her arms as if that would somehow provide a barrier between them. 'I was going to knock him out.'

'Tell me something,' he said conversationally, moving closer to her. 'Did you dress up specially for the occasion? Is that why you're wearing that extraordinary judo outfit?'

'They're pyjamas,' she answered stubbornly, her throat constricting as she realised they were much more clinging than she had bargained for.

'Uh-huh,' he drawled, nodding. 'And where did you train—the Ninja turtle school of self-defence? I'll bet you're a sixth Dan, at least.'

Her hands crept to her face, and she could feel it hot under her fingers.

'Don't be ridiculous,' she snapped, her chin lifting. 'They're pyjamas. *You* bought them for me.'

'Did I?' he drawled. 'I can't think why.'

'To sleep in, I imagine,' she replied shortly, trying to sound cool and realising she'd forgotten how to breathe.

'What an amazing idea,' he said softly, putting the wine bottle on the table and taking another step towards her. 'But I didn't choose them. As far as I'm concerned, wearing clothes in bed is a shocking waste of time.'

The way he was looking at her was too much. She wanted to run away and run towards him, all at the same time. Her heart seemed to be beating in her throat, and she wanted to say something smart but her brain seemed suddenly to have cut off.

The only thing that existed here and now was the way Finn was looking at her.

She stared at him mutely as the light glowed on her face and throat, her stomach clenching as she gazed at his expression. And then suddenly he had reached out and she was in his arms, his hands sliding under the silk and over her skin, his lips on her lips. It was...heaven, Cara thought. It was what heaven had to be like.

She had no reason, no explanation why this should be so right, except that she knew it was. And that she never wanted it to end.

And then like a cold wind on a warm day, her whole body stilled as he stopped. She opened her eyes and saw mirrored in his the aching desire she felt. But there was something else, too, a look she didn't want to recognise, a look that she could read only as disgust.

And before she could say anything he had dropped his arms and was pulling away from her, as if the very feel of her burnt him.

'This is madness,' he said. 'Utter bloody madness.'

She stared at him in mute disbelief, noting the grim set of his face, and the fevered magic of the moment shattered like thin crystal. Stifling a cry, she ran to her room and slammed the door behind her.

'Cara?' Finn stood in her doorway, looking at her as she lay on her bed. She didn't even have to turn her head to see what he was doing. She had heard the door open and she could imagine exactly how he looked, standing on the threshold with the light of the hall behind him.

She heard his light steps and then the shift of the mattress as he sat next to her. 'Go away,' she spat.

'I know you're upset with me,' he said. 'And for what it's worth, I'm sorry.'

She hugged herself into a tighter ball. The look in his eyes was something that had cut her more deeply than she cared to admit, even to herself.

He put his hand on her shoulder, and she flinched at the sudden shaft of helpless desire it triggered. She swallowed and steeled herself not to let him affect her this way. 'Go away,' she repeated. 'I'm not...I'm not interested in your...sexual advances.' The words sounded ridiculous to her ears, and she waited for him to laugh, wondering with a thudding pulse what she would do if he simply ignored her.

Instead his hand lifted away, and there was a little silence. 'I'm sorry, Cara,' he repeated. 'I'm sorry I've upset you, but right now I haven't got time to explain. There are more important things for you to worry about at the moment.'

His words were so unexpected she rolled over and stared at him. 'Like what?'

He looked at her expressionlessly. It was as if the man who had set her alight a few moments before had never existed. 'I'm afraid you're going to have to get dressed again,' he said. 'We're leaving.'

She stared at him. 'Leaving? In the middle of the night? What for?'

Finn sighed, reached for her hand and began to run his fingers over her knuckles, just like he had done all that time ago when they first met. Yesterday.

And again, after the first startled moment of contact, she didn't pull her hand away.

'I didn't want to tell you my doubts earlier,' he said at last. 'Because I thought it was probably nothing. But now I've been for a look round, I've made my mind up.'

'About what?' she demanded.

'Cara,' he asked, 'what exactly does the phrase safe house mean to you?'

She shrugged, momentarily off balance at his question. 'Somewhere we can be safe.'

He nodded slowly, his eyes holding hers. 'Somewhere with protection, wouldn't you say?'

She stared at him, not liking the implications of what he was saying, not in the slightest bit.

'You see,' he said softly, 'we haven't got any protection here at all. And the telephone is out of order.'

'But the police—' she began.

'Told me there would be people guarding the house.' He nodded. 'Well, there aren't any. I've just checked. Nothing. Not even signs that anyone has been here. Mind you—' he shrugged '—there's no sign of Luca, either.'

'You mean we could have been set up?' she demanded, her eyes widening. 'That someone in the police might be working for Luca?'

He nodded slowly. 'That's about the size of it, yes.' He dropped her hand, got up and made for the doorway, pausing with his hand on the jamb. 'It could be nothing,' he said again, before disappearing towards his room. 'But I'm not taking any chances.'

She sat up in bed, staring at the space where he had been for ten seconds, thinking about what had happened between them in the kitchen. He had seemed genuinely sorry to have upset her, that was the confusing thing.

Nothing about him was like Luca at all. And Luca was her only real point of reference.

Luca. She had to fight the panic at the idea of what he would do if he caught them. In one jerky movement, she got up and began dressing hurriedly.

In not many more seconds, it seemed, they had packed, locked up and were once more in the car.

Cara unwound her window, looking at the star-strung sky and then at the countryside, bathed in moon shadow. 'Luca's somewhere out there,' she breathed and felt a sudden chill, in spite of the warm night air. She understood the panic-stricken urge of a stampeding animal. Without even realising it she pressed her feet against the floor of the car, as if willing it to go faster.

'You can push all you like,' drawled Finn. 'But we won't get away any quicker.' He smiled as she glanced at him and she knew he could tell exactly what she was thinking.

'I can't help it,' she whispered. 'I can't—'

He lifted a hand off the gear stick and reached for one of hers. 'Yes, you can,' he contradicted her. 'Remember, one step at a time on that high wire, and don't look down. We'll get out of this, I promise you.'

And smiling encouragingly at her, he took the brake off and began coasting down the track to the road.

Nobody shot at them or leapt out at them from behind a tree, as Cara kept expecting. At the junction Finn took a good look round, then put his foot down and headed for the open road as if he was driving in a grand prix.

'Lights!' yelped Cara. 'We haven't got any lights on!'

'We don't want any yet,' Finn told her, concentrating hard on the road ahead. 'If anybody's watching, the more confusion we can sow, the better.'

But after half a mile or so, he did switch the lights on, and Cara breathed again. 'Where are we?' she asked, relief flooding her body at the idea they were once more out of any possible danger for however short a time.

He glanced sidewise at her. 'I haven't the faintest idea,' he replied.

He smiled at the expression on her face and turned to the road. 'Okay. In general terms we're in Provence, as you know. But the country roads here are so twisty, it's a job to have an exact idea without a map and a couple of road signs.'

'Are we going to drive all night?' she demanded.

'Are you ever going to stop asking questions?' he countered.

She glared at him, and then as his expression didn't alter, she sat back discontentedly in her seat, folded her arms and stared out the windscreen. 'I can't help asking questions,' she remarked at last to no one in particular. 'I always do when I'm nervous.'

'Here's a question for you, then,' said Finn softly, staring intently in the rear-view mirror. 'Did it ever occur to you that I might be nervous, too?'

Cara stared at him blankly, and as his eyes slid to hers he grinned suddenly. It made his face look years younger, as if suddenly she could see what he must have been like as a boy. 'I'll take that look of amazement as a compliment,' he said conversationally.

'I—' Cara stopped. She remembered how only the day before he had made some flippant remark when she asked him if he ever worried about anything.

But it had really been a rhetorical question on her part. The truth was she had never actually thought about Finn's feelings at all, apart from how he might feel about her. 'You never seem nervous,' she said lamely at last.

She thought of the way he had stopped her wedding, then fended off Luca with that chocolate gun. 'I would never think of you as being scared of anything,' she added in surprise.

He flashed her a look she didn't understand at all. 'We're all scared of something,' he said quietly.

'What...what are you scared of?' she asked as bravely as she could. Something told her that this was a territory where Finn didn't welcome invaders. Still, he had brought up the subject.

He looked at her expressionlessly, then turned his attention once more to the road ahead. 'I guess I'm scared of the past catching up with me,' he said at last, and there was a grim finality to his tone that made her close her mouth and turn away to look once more at the dark countryside rushing past her window.

Time passed in silence between them, each busy with their own thoughts. However, it was Finn who spoke first. 'We'll stay at an *auberge* tonight,' he told her. 'But I think we ought to make quite sure first that there is no one following us.'

And then he cut the engine and his lights and coasted into a lay-by, finally coming to a halt under a tree in the deepest shadow he could find.

They seemed to sit there for hours. 'Was it the police who betrayed us?' Cara asked at last.

Finn shrugged. 'It would only need one person,' he said. 'I trust my contact, and we have to believe the police are still hunting Luca. But it will be safer if, from now on, we act as if we are on our own.'

Cara thought of her uncle and Luca, and for the first time began to try to think objectively about them. But it was almost impossible.

She remembered the presents her uncle had given her when she was small, the way she had been completely taken care of. His kindness and affection. On the other hand, she had to admit, he had completely ignored her plea for help at the marriage ceremony.

And Luca, for all that he had a brutal personality, liked to listen to opera. He gave lavishly to charity, too, she remembered. He had been a bully as a boy, but had always protected her in squabbles with other playmates. In later years she had often got comfort from this, assuming it meant he must have some hidden tenderness. Now she was not so sure. To Luca, she realised, she was simply his exclusive property.

None of this meant they were crooks, though, or that anything Finn said about them was true. Especially when she knew absolutely nothing about Finn.

She opened her mouth to question him, but he held up his hand, listening. And then in the distance she could hear it, as well. A car labouring up the steep gradient of the twisty road. 'It could be tourists,' she breathed. 'Or some local farmer staggering back from a bar.'

He nodded without saying anything, then opened the door and slid out. She could see him spreading his jacket over the car's rear reflectors, then disappearing in the shadow. The car was coming closer and closer, its headlights searching through the sky then levelling out as it reached the top of the gradient. Without exactly knowing why, she slid down in her seat. What on earth was Finn up to out there?

Then in a rush the car was coming past. For a moment it seemed to slow, then, gathering speed, it roared past and away on up the road. Cara breathed a shaky sigh and bit back a scream when the car door opened. It was Finn.

'That was Luca,' he said, almost unnecessarily. 'Alfa Romeo, Italian number plates and old bullet head himself at the wheel.'

'He has not got a bullet head,' snapped Cara unthinkingly, and then, seeing Finn's surprised face, shrugged irritably. 'Well, okay, maybe a bit of one,' she amended.

'Why, after all he's done to you, do you keep sticking up for him?' Finn demanded.

'I've spent my life making excuses for him,' she answered at last. 'He's always upset people, ever since I can remember. And it just always fell to me to smooth things over. It's a difficult habit to break.'

He gazed at her sardonically and took the handbrake off. 'Remind me to recommend you for a job as chief diplomat at the UN when we get out of this,' he said.

'What are we doing now?' she demanded as they began to coast down the mountain.

'I would have thought that was obvious,' he replied.

'Nothing's obvious,' she snapped. 'Except for the fact you haven't started the engine, we still have no lights on, and we're going down a mountain with about three million hairpin bends.'

'Yes, well, apart from that,' he drawled, and then glancing at her face, added, 'if you had been listening carefully back there, you would have heard Luca stop shortly after he went past us. He probably went back to the lay-by to check if we were there and is now jumping up and down, upsetting a few more members of his entourage.' He glanced at her. 'Want to go back and smooth things over?'

That drive was something Cara never wanted to remember and could never forget. Stopping and starting, coasting down treacherous roads that were more high up than she cared to think about, bends that a careless driver wouldn't see until he was hurtling through them and into the thin air above seemingly bottomless ravines.

But Finn was not careless. At the beginning she stopped herself once or twice from telling him he was imagining things, but then in the thrumming silence of the night she, too, could hear the faint note of a car coming after them.

It was not until about two hours later that he seemed to relax and turn off the road at a signpost to an old stone *auberge*.

'It's too late,' objected Cara, looking worriedly at the shuttered building as they drove round the back. 'Everybody'll be in bed.'

Finn merely shot her a look as he parked the car in an old barn. 'Well, I'll just have to use that famous charm of mine, won't I?' he said smoothly as he got out of the car. 'Are you coming, or not?'

She stumbled wearily in his wake as he walked across the yard and knocked at the very solid-looking oak door. 'You won't be able to charm them if they're in bed,' she muttered waspishly, and wondered if it was possible to sleep standing up.

But to her intense surprise, within a few minutes, the door was opened a crack and then thrown wide before Finn was enveloped in the embrace of a very large and smiling French woman.

'A fan of yours, I take it,' said Cara, yawning, as she followed Finn into the dim hall.

'Actually, it's more that I am a fan of hers and her husband,' replied Finn. 'Marie and Henri have been very good to me over the years.'

He went with them to the little cubby-hole under the stairs that served as a reception desk, while Cara sank gratefully onto a chair.

She was totally unprepared a few moments later for the woman to rush across to her, lift her bodily into her arms and kiss her soundly on both cheeks.

And she was out of her depth in the flood of French that followed.

'What's going on?' she asked feebly. 'Are we the first guests they've had in years, or something?'

Finn looked at her deadpan. 'She's congratulating you on your marriage,' he said, beginning to climb the stairs.

'I didn't get married,' said Cara, as the woman patted her cheek and then let her follow him. 'Remember?'

'Not that marriage,' he said expressionlessly. 'Ours.'

She stopped on the stairs and her heart stilled at what he had just said. She must have misheard. 'What did you say?' she demanded.

'You heard,' he replied, turning out of sight at the top of the landing.

Cara looked back to see Marie and Henri standing together at the bottom of the stairs. They were both beaming at her, and she nodded helplessly at them before scuttling in Finn's wake.

He was standing by the door of a tiny room dominated by a double bed. It was very high and overstuffed. But the rough sheets were spotlessly clean, and there was a bowl of dried lavender on the window sill.

'Is this some kind of a joke?' she demanded as she got up close.

'No,' he replied tersely.

She walked into the room and turned to face him. 'Tell me if I'm wrong,' she said. 'But I distinctly got the impression you said *our* marriage.'

He folded his arms and leant against the only other piece of furniture in the room—a wardrobe with a definite list to one side. 'I did,' he said wearily. 'It seemed the most sensible thing to do in the circumstances, especially when the only other room available is right at the other end of the *auberge*—well out of earshot if Luca called and I wanted you to come to my rescue.'

He smiled faintly and spread his hands in a gesture that was very French. 'They just seemed to take it for granted that we would be sharing. And when Marie saw your engagement ring, she put two and two together and made five.'

Cara looked at the diamond ring on her third finger. The gem was so large, so ostentatious she generally wore it with the stone on the inside of her hand. Anyone looking at her fingers could mistake it for a wedding ring.

Finn put a hand out and touched her gently on the cheek. 'I'm sorry I've got you into this situation, Cara,' he said.

'I don't know what you mean,' she replied as coolly as she could, his touch making her pulse thud once more. Why couldn't she control the way her body reacted to him?

He stared expressionlessly at her for a moment. 'Yes, you do,' he said quietly, his hand dropping to his side. He sighed and sat on the bed. 'It's okay,' he said, rubbing his jaw wearily. 'You needn't worry that I'm going to try anything on.'

'I don't know what you're talking about,' she retorted quickly, too quickly. She stalked to the window and stirred the lavender with her fingers, the heady perfume filling the small room. 'You're so arrogant,' she blurted. 'Why should you ever think I'd let you?'

'Because you're very attracted to me,' he said simply.

She whirled round, her face flaming, lavender spattering on the polished wooden floorboards. He was gazing at her quite calmly, undoing the top buttons of his shirt and looking totally at home. Looking, Cara thought with a sudden flash of fury, as though they were discussing what they'd had for dinner. 'You're so arrogant,' she repeated, trying not to let her eyes follow his fingers as they moved down his chest, fluidly undoing each button.

Finn shrugged. 'So you keep saying.' He looked at her again and held her gaze. 'But I'm right, aren't I?'

'No!' she snapped.

CHAPTER SEVEN

CARA knew she was turning crimson, and there was nothing she could do about it. 'You . . . you were the one who kissed me,' she accused, floundering before those eyes that missed nothing. 'You led me to this point. All I wanted to do was get away from my wedding.'

He was undoing the buttons of his cuffs, his long brown fingers dextrous against the blue cotton.

'And the look in your eyes when I kissed you in Monte Carlo?' he inquired. 'Where did that come from?' He shook his head. 'I agree we've been thrown together, but you are a very beautiful woman, Cara. I would be lying if I said I wasn't attracted to you.'

'You . . . you are?' she replied uncertainly, thinking of the way he had pushed her away in the safe house. 'I...I don't believe you,' she said in a rush. 'I think I'm just like an interesting toy to you. You pick me up, find out exactly how I work and then put me down and go on to something else.'

He smiled at her, and she felt her knees turn to jelly. 'You are such an intriguing woman,' he said softly.

'Don't you mean specimen?' she retorted.

He shook his head. 'Why cast me as an ogre?' he demanded softly. 'I'm the one who's trying to act honourably. I'm the one who's trying very hard not to pick you up and then put you down again.'

'Do you want me to thank you?' she snapped.

He looked at her lazily. 'If you like,' he replied. 'It's a pretty superhuman effort on my part.'

116

She glared at him and could think of absolutely nothing to say. But she had to say something. She couldn't let him get away with . . . whatever it was he was getting away with. 'Huh!' she snorted at last.

He suppressed a smile. 'You know, you have a charm that for once in my life I simply cannot define,' he drawled. 'But what really intrigues me about you is that you seem to have simply no idea how beautiful you are. Now why do you find that so difficult to believe?'

'I don't know,' she said shortly, still cross with him. 'Maybe nobody's ever said it to me before.'

He looked so astonished she felt herself going hot with embarrassment. 'Nobody?' he echoed.

She shrugged irritably, wanting to change the subject and not knowing how. 'My uncle said often that I was pretty, and Cesarina, our housekeeper, said so, too. But I suppose I didn't meet that many people who weren't either family or business friends of my uncle and Luca.' She paused, thinking. 'They sometimes would look at me in a certain way,' she conceded. 'But hardly any would speak to me. And if they did, Luca got terribly angry.'

'And what about Luca?' he asked. 'Didn't he tell you that you were beautiful?'

She shook her head. She didn't want to talk about herself. She wanted Finn to talk about his life, to tell her about that past that he kept locked up behind those eyes of his. 'I . . . I don't think so,' she replied at last, frowning with the effort of trying to remember what she and Luca had ever talked about.

He raised an eyebrow. 'You don't think so?' he echoed.

'Well—' she shrugged '—I don't know what it is about him, but every time he started talking I just used to switch off. I couldn't help it. It got me into terrible trouble sometimes. Maybe he said it when I wasn't listening.' She shrugged self-consciously. 'I doubt it, though,' she added, faltering. 'I was just a piece of property to him.'

There was a look on Finn's face she couldn't read at all, and she gazed at him speechlessly as he reached for her hand and held it to his lips. 'You only need to look in a mirror to see how beautiful you are,' he said softly.

She thought of the way the policewoman had looked at him in the hotel and dragged her hand from his. 'I bet you've said that to lots of women.' She forced the words out.

He smiled and then seeing her face, said, 'Actually, no.'

She squashed a sudden irrational hopefulness and looked him square in the eye. 'No?' she drawled as scathingly as she could.

He shook his head. 'No. Most of the women I've been out with spend half their lives looking in a mirror. They know down to the last invisible wrinkle exactly how they look.'

There was a sudden grim look on his face that made her feel rather sorry for his girlfriends.

'It doesn't matter what someone looks like,' she said stiffly. 'It only matters what they are told they look like by the people they love.'

He looked at her and smiled a little bitterly. 'Very Italian,' he remarked. 'But I'm not sure about the truth of that remark. I haven't loved anybody for a long time.'

There was a little silence, and he sighed and then gazed seriously at her. 'And I'm not going to say I love you, Cara, so don't hold your breath—because it would just be a lie.'

Her mouth opened at the unexpectedness of his harsh words but he swept on. 'I don't want to hurt you, and

I know I could, so I might as well be honest. For the first time in my life I'm going to do the decent thing.' He shrugged. 'I guess that means you can have the bed to yourself. You look beat. I'll sleep on the floor.'

'If you're sure,' she heard herself saying, and then blushed as he glanced at her. 'I mean,' she added hurriedly, 'I could sleep on the floor, I suppose. You're the one who's been under most of the strain, what with driving and everything. . . .' She trailed off, knowing that she was gabbling.

There was silence between them, and as Cara gazed at Finn she felt her heart contract at the tiredness etched on his face. 'You look like you could do with a good rest,' she said softly.

He lay back on the bed, his hands clasped behind his head. 'Yes, I suppose I could,' he admitted. 'But I don't want to sleep in tomorrow,' he added, staring at the ceiling. 'I want you to wake me, okay?' He yawned. 'We need to contact the police as early as we can and find out what is going on.'

Cara crossed to the wash basin, filled it with warm water and began to wash her face and neck. It felt so good, so comforting, after all those hot, anxious hours in the car.

The mirror above the basin was old and losing its silver backing in places, but there was enough to reflect her face, to show that her eyes looked darker than normal, the pupils a soft black in the green-flecked irises.

For the first time in her life she was sharing a room with a man, a man she hardly knew at all, and her heart was pounding. The fact that the man was Finn was neither here nor there, she told herself sternly. But it had taken more than a little bravado to do something as silly as wash her face in front of him.

Maybe she should have gone somewhere else, found a bathroom, but it had been almost a point of honour to show how little she was affected by him. How empty his arrogant assumptions about her were.

But then she thought of the way he had touched her in the safe house, and her pulse skittered out of control once more. Reaching with studied calm for a towel, she turned to Finn, but whatever she had been going to say died on her lips. He was fast asleep.

She opened her mouth and then, looking at his face, closed it again. If anybody needed a good night's sleep, he did.

However, he was not going to get one, she realised, in that position. Since he had just leaned back and dozed off, it was all too obvious that he was either going to slide right off the mattress into an untidy heap on the floor, or he might just roll over and simply fall off.

Somehow she would have to pull him up so he was lying properly.

She looked at his prone form for a few seconds, and suddenly, from the depths of her memory, she remembered the face of the man who years ago had delivered her uncle's grand piano—and had been told to take it upstairs. She had laughed then, as she had scurried about to get him some help. But now... She gazed at Finn. Now she knew exactly how he felt.

He was so big, and he looked so relaxed. And what would happen if he woke up? Trying hard to ignore a quick flutter in her heart, she stepped up to the bed, and with more stealth than she knew she possessed, she undid his shoes and eased them off.

Then she clambered carefully onto the soft springiness of the bed and knelt behind his head. Putting her hands gingerly under his arms, she attempted to lift him farther up the mattress, but with absolutely no success.

She was going to be absolutely stuck if he woke up, she thought with a nervous jolt. And what would he say? Something horribly sarcastic, no doubt. She stared at him crossly. He had no right to look so peaceful. He was actually smiling, blast him.

She sighed gustily and bit her lip. For such a lean-looking man, he was much heavier than she had bargained for, and it didn't help that the bed was so soft. It was as difficult to manouevre in as quicksand.

Still, she thought doggedly, she couldn't just leave him where he was. He had to be really uncomfortable in that position, even though he was still smiling. How could anyone look so relaxed in such an awkward shape?

She thought of all he had done for her, and set her jaw. Finn deserved a proper sleep, and a proper sleep was what he was going to get. Gritting her teeth, she grasped his arms once more and pulled.

This time his shirt came away in her hands and he muttered indistinctly in his sleep. She stilled where she was, wondering again how she was going to explain herself if he did suddenly wake up.

Then, dropping the shirt on the floor, she slid her fingers under his arms once more, trying hard to disregard how smooth and beguiling his skin felt, how beautifully proportioned his body was, his wide shoulders tapering to a narrow waist and the play of muscles against her hands.

After what seemed centuries but must have been only a few minutes, his body seemed to obey Cara's ineffectual tugging and moved up the bed. With one last effort, she lifted his head and shoved a pillow underneath it.

For a split second she thought of taking his trousers off, and then shied away from the idea. It would certainly make him more comfortable, but if he woke up while that was going on, she thought with a shudder, she really wouldn't have a leg to stand on. She pictured the scene and clenched her fists. No. She simply didn't have the bravado to carry it off.

She knelt by him, everything they had done together running through her mind like a videotape, and then she leant over his face, studying it as she could never do when he was awake. His eyelashes were thick and dark, and his nose was lovely, long and straight.

Without quite knowing what she was doing she reached out a forefinger to trace his lips, his chin, the point on his cheek where she was sure he had a dimple. But at that exact moment his eyes snapped open and he stared at her.

She bit back a gasp and snatched away her fingers. 'It's not time to wake up yet,' she quavered softly. 'Go to sleep.'

He turned on his side and slid his arms around her, pulling her down beside him. 'No, Finn,' she remonstrated, but it was too late. His eyes had closed once more and his face was nuzzling the warmth of her throat. Tentatively she tried to move away, but his arms pulled her closer. It was no good, she realised, his arm resting on her as heavy as a bar of lead. She couldn't get away without waking him.

She looked at the floor and thought how hard it would be as a bed. Maybe she would just stay here with Finn and then move to the floor before he woke up. That way, they'd both have a good night's sleep. It was really a very sensible solution. Especially since, with any luck, he'd never know what she'd done. With a sigh she pulled the light cord above the bed, and within seconds she, too, was fast asleep.

A rooster was crowing somewhere in the streaky dawn when she opened her eyes and saw Finn lying next to her. He looked as though he had collapsed straight on the bed and fallen asleep, just like that. But then, she thought muzzily, that was what he had done. He was facing her, and her heart contracted at the unexpected boyishness of his face, the grim lines smoothed away by sleep.

As she tugged at one of the blankets to spread it over him his arm drew her close once more. 'Don't,' she whispered. But he was fast asleep again, a faint smile on his face. There was something that she had meant to wake up for, she thought sleepily, but then, her arms cradling him, she dozed off once more.

When Cara surfaced again, the sunshine was flooding in through their window. There was a warmth, a feeling of constriction around her body she was not used to. Blinking her eyes fully open, she realised that Finn's arms were around her, his face buried in a sheaf of hair on the nape of her neck.

Hurriedly she tried to move away before he woke up, but his arms only tightened about her and pulled her closer. He mumbled something sleepily, kissed her and then there was silence once more.

Her heart was beating fast. Why on earth had she thought that sharing a bed with Finn would be a good idea? It was like cuddling up with a sleeping tiger. And what was she going to do when he woke up? She remembered waking at dawn and groaned. If only she had got up when she planned.

She tried once more to move away from him, but it was no use, she was held fast. If anything, he tightened his grip, and she tried to stop the way her heart bounced crazily as his hand slid over her stomach.

'This is a nice way to wake up,' a sleepy voice behind her murmured.

Cara turned immediately to face him. 'No, it's not,' she answered, 'and you're not to get the wrong idea,' she added hurriedly, trying and failing once more to extricate herself from his arms.

She had hoped that he would look wildly unattractive when he was half asleep, that maybe the sight of his hair standing up on end or his stubbly chin would put her completely off. But if anything, she realised with a thudding heart, his sleepiness merely added to his charm. It was preposterous the way he could affect her. Simply preposterous.

'Let me go,' she snapped exasperatedly. 'Do you hear?'

His eyes snapped fully open, looking straight into hers, and she could feel herself reddening at his gaze. 'Well, this is much better than waking up on the floor,' he drawled. 'Tell me,' he added silkily. 'How exactly did I get here?'

Cara's mouth opened but he swept on reflectively, 'You know, I don't think I've ever been carried to a woman's bed before. If I'd known you were going to be so assertive I'd have stayed awake a bit longer.'

'I didn't carry you,' she bit out. 'You lay back on the bed and fell asleep. I just…' She swallowed. 'I just pulled you up a bit.'

He looked at her completely innocently, his body moving so that he cradled her head in the crook of his arm. 'That's your story,' he drawled, his fingers stroking her cheek. 'But how am I to know you didn't take advantage of me?'

Her lips parted, and he kissed them softly. The blood was pounding in her ears at his closeness, his tone, his touch. 'You...you know that's ridiculous,' she forced out.

Finn pulled back a little, his lips curving. 'You have such a powerful way of boosting my ego,' he drawled mockingly.

'I didn't mean...' she began confusedly. 'I meant—'

'So tell me,' he interrupted, looking at her. 'How come half my clothes are missing?'

She bit her lip. 'I took them off,' she said, adding hurriedly, 'you looked uncomfortable. I thought I was doing you a favour.'

The glint in his eye was only too obvious. 'I must try that line sometime,' he said thoughtfully. 'Unfortunately, I don't think there are too many women who'd buy it.'

His free hand pushed through her hair and traced a path down her throat. It was difficult to think of anything except the way he was looking at her. Impossible not to want him, the way she knew he wanted her.

'So did we have a wild night of passion?' he asked deadpan. 'Or not? And do you normally make love with all your clothes on?' he inquired. 'I want to know all about it.'

He was unzipping her dress, stripping it away from her with a relaxed ease that she simply couldn't resist. That, if she was honest with herself, she didn't want to resist.

His fingers stroked over her skin, unhooking her bra, her breath catching as his hands slid round her breasts, touching and teasing their hardening peaks.

'No,' she gasped, attempting to answer his question. 'I've...I've never made love at all.'

And then suddenly, he stared at her as if seeing her properly for the first time. His fingers stilled and he pulled away as if he had been stung.

She gazed at him in shock. It was the same way he had treated her the evening before, taking her in his arms and then rejecting her as if she was pure poison. She felt frozen, confused, see-sawingly uncertain as he fell back on his side of the bed, staring at the ceiling, his hands under his head.

Cara stared at him for a few thudding seconds, then scrambled as far away as she could get from him, pulling the sheets with her.

'Why did you do that?' she demanded. 'Was it just to show you could?'

He turned his head to her. 'It was because I wanted to,' he said.

Tears were filling her eyes. 'Then why did you stop?' she whispered. 'Why are you doing this to me?'

'I stopped because I'm trying not to do anything to you,' he snapped.

He was so good-looking, lying there against the crumpled white sheets. She could see the muscles in his arms bunch slightly as he moved his hands under his head. She fought down the impulse to reach out and touch the strong column of his throat, his unshaven chin, the high planes of his cheeks.

And then she realized he was looking at her as minutely as she was staring at him. She could feel herself flush at his gaze, the colour rising up her neck and flooding her face.

She clasped her hands. 'Is it because of who I am?' she asked at last.

He sighed and put his hand over both of hers. 'No, Cara,' he said gently. 'It's because of what you are.'

She stared at him. 'Because I've never made love before?' She forced the words out.

'Yes.' He nodded. 'Partly.'

'Why?' she persisted. 'Why should it make a difference? Surely everybody has to make love some time or other?'

He laughed a little at that, and she glared at him. 'Don't,' she said shortly. 'And I don't see what's so funny.'

'Cara,' he said softly. 'When you make love for the first time, it should be with a man who means a lot to you, who loves you. Someone you want to spend your whole life with.'

She shrugged uncertainly. 'I was expected to make love with Luca and I wouldn't want to spend five minutes with him now,' she replied at last.

His face tightened, but his voice remained calm. 'You're on the run from a man you were within a whisker of marrying,' he said at last. 'You can't really feel anything for me.' His jaw tightened. 'There simply hasn't been enough time.'

His hand was still on hers, warm and oddly comforting in spite of the harsh edge to his words. She lifted her chin. 'I didn't...' She swallowed and went on with a studied coolness she didn't feel. 'I didn't know that there was a set timetable for feelings, Finn. What would you like me to do? Make an appointment to come back later?'

He looked as though he wanted to say several things all at once, but instead he turned from her suddenly and punched his pillow into shape. 'You don't know anything about me,' he chided, lying back and staring at her with that direct gaze that seemed to see everything. 'And I'm not the kind of man a girl like you really wants to know that well.'

'What does that make Luca?' she asked bitterly.

He looked at her grimly. 'In some ways, I'm much worse than Luca.'

Her lips parted in astonishment. 'Worse than Luca?' she echoed. 'That's not possible.'

'Okay, so maybe I've got better table manners than him,' he drawled with a bitter edge to his voice that took all the humour out of his words. 'But I'm definitely not the kind of guy you want to get into bed with.' His lips twisted. 'It's not that I don't like you, Cara,' he added. 'It's just that I don't want any commitments, and I don't want to hurt you.'

She flashed a look at him. 'And what about what you said yesterday?' she demanded. 'In the hotel in Monte Carlo, when you kissed me. You said we both knew how we felt about each other. You...' She paused and then rushed on. 'You wanted me then.'

His hand tightened on hers as his face set grimly. 'That was yesterday,' he said. 'Before I came to my senses.'

'Well, thank you for informing me,' she retorted, stung more than she cared to admit by his words. 'It was very reasonable of you.'

Finn held her eyes with his and shook his head. 'I'm not the man for you, Cara,' he said at last. 'I only ever loved one woman before, and I broke her heart. I'm not about to go through that again. I like women, don't get me wrong. But every relationship I have is strictly temporary.'

'Why's that?' Cara demanded. 'Because you're scared?' She gasped as she realised what she had just said. 'I'm sorry,' she gabbled, not wanting to meet his eye. 'That was wrong of me.'

She looked up and was shocked to see the pain etched on his face. 'Yes, it was,' he said. 'But it was all a long time ago. And she's dead. So what does any of it matter?'

He sat up suddenly and swung his legs to the floor. 'I need a shower,' he said abruptly.

'It matters to me,' muttered Cara, trying and failing to look away from the long, muscled length of his body. She put out a hand to him. 'Finn,' she pleaded. 'Wait.'

He looked her straight in the eye. 'For what?'

She pulled back her hand at the iciness in his tone. 'What...what was her name?' she asked at last. 'The woman who loved you?'

He stared at her consideringly for a few seconds. 'Louise,' he said at last. 'And I killed her.'

Cara's whole body stilled at the brutality of his words. 'You killed her?' she whispered. 'Like...like you say Luca—'

'Like I say Luca gets rid of people?' he finished for her. 'No. I was altogether more cruel than he would ever be.' He shook his head and sighed. 'I was too young and too stupid to see what I was doing, I suppose. I treated her very badly, and she killed herself.'

'What happened?' Cara whispered.

'I don't want to talk about it,' he said roughly.

'You never want to talk about anything,' she snapped.

He turned slowly to gaze at her with a look that would have stripped paint. 'What did you say?' he asked with dangerous calmness.

Cara pulled the sheets more securely round her and then met his eyes, her chin up.

'I said,' she began, trying hard to sound cool, 'that you never want to talk about anything. Anything im-

portant. You just erect these walls round yourself with
big signs stuck on them, saying Do Not Enter, Help Not
Wanted.'

His eyes didn't waver from her face, and she could
feel herself going pink.

'You're taking a very big risk, you know,' he said
quietly.

'I don't care,' she said weakly. 'I'm beginning to get
used to taking them.'

He was still staring at her, and then as she dropped
her gaze, he nodded slowly. 'Yes, I guess you are,' he
agreed.

'I mean,' she said quickly, 'you know all about me,
and I know nothing about you.'

'What do you want to know?' he asked matter-of-
factly.

Cara's mind went completely blank at this unexpected
directness. She clasped her hands and then unclasped
them. This wasn't how it was meant to be, at all. 'You
mean, I can just ask you?' she said. 'Anything?'

'I didn't say I'd necessarily answer you,' he drawled,
his face absolutely deadpan. 'What exactly do you want
to know? My address? I live in Manhattan. Birthday?
June twenty-first. Telephone number? Ex-directory.
What else?'

'Well,' she began uncertainly, 'I mean, you know, in
the movies . . . and books, when people get to know each
other, they just tell each other things. It's . . . it's not like
a job interview. I—' She floundered. 'I thought . . .'

He leant back against the pillows once more. 'You
thought that in the darkness of the night, I might be so
overcome by my feelings for you that I would feel I
simply had to tell you all about the tragic moments of
my life, and then I would feel so grateful for unbur-

dening myself that I would reach out to you, like this.'
His hand slid round her arm and drew her close so she
was lying against his chest.

'And then I would kiss you, like this.' His head bent
to hers, his lips tasting the sweet moisture of her mouth.

For one glorious, beautiful moment, his touch was all
she needed to remember how much he could make her
feel. And then at the memory of his cold cynicism, fury
began to move through her veins. This was not how it
was meant to be at all.

She began to pound at his chest, tearing herself from
his fingers until his hold on her relaxed. Rubbing her
lips with her hand, she sat back and glared at him. 'How
dare you do that!' she spat. 'How dare you make fun
of me like that!'

His chest was rising and falling as though he had been
in a race, and he looked at her bleakly. 'I don't know,'
he said at last. 'But if it's any consolation, it affected
me rather more than I bargained for.'

'Am I supposed to feel sorry for you?' she snapped.
'When you obviously don't give a damn about me?'

He reached for her, then pulled away abruptly. 'For
God's sake, Cara,' he said urgently. 'I can't . . . we can't
do this.'

She stared at him, wondering at the real turmoil he
was in. 'Why not?' she asked simply.

He looked at her for a long moment. 'You must be
out of your mind,' he said at last. 'No. Correction. I
must be out of mine.'

She looked at him and swallowed hard. Perhaps she
had been wrong about the way he felt for her. 'Do I
disgust you so much?' she asked.

'Disgust?' he echoed in amazement, before shaking
his head. 'I disgust myself,' he said. 'The only thing I

want to do is get you out of this mess in one piece and then—'

'Go?' she supplied. Did she really mean so little to him?

'I'm not the kind of man who would make you happy,' he said grimly, sitting up once more. 'I'm ten years older than you, and there are times when I feel like it could be a hundred.'

He looked at her, sitting perfectly still on her side of the bed, then he stared at his feet. 'You know nothing of life outside that gilded cage you were brought up in,' he added. 'I'm probably the first man outside your family you've ever spoken more than two words to.'

Her hands twisted in the sheet, and she forced herself to meet his gaze. 'How you must despise me,' she said at last, in a low voice. 'Here I am, this stupid little girl, throwing myself at a man she hardly knows.' She reached for her dress and wondered if it was possible to feel more miserable than she was already feeling. She suddenly wanted to run away, anywhere. Even back to Luca would be better than this kind of torture.

'It's not like that,' he told her.

'Oh, no?' She stopped and looked at him. 'You needn't be kind to me,' she said coolly. 'Just to spare my feelings. I know I've acted ridiculously. I won't... compromise you again.'

He gazed at her steadily. 'You're putting that dress on back to front,' he drawled.

She thrust her head through the neck hole and glared at him. 'Damn you, Finn,' she snapped. 'Just leave me alone, all right?'

'No,' he said. 'It's not all right. You're not going to start whipping yourself into an agony of self-pity just because of me.'

Her jaw dropped. 'You—' she began, but he swept on.

'For a start,' he said, 'you're one of the most attractive women I've ever met. God dammit, I *like* kissing you. Sometimes it seems the most natural thing in the world to do.'

But Cara was past listening. 'You made me feel like I've never felt before,' she raged at him, wildly feeling about for an armhole. 'And when I finally realise how much I'm attracted to you, you turn round and say…no thanks, I'm doing the honourable thing.

'I can imagine how you will laugh when you go back to America,' she snapped. 'Oh, yes, you'll tell your friends, I took this girl from her wedding, right in the middle of the ceremony. And I put her under a spell, just like that. Just like I do with every other woman I meet.' Cara swallowed hurriedly, sorting out the tangle of her dress, and savagely pulled it straight.

'And then, you know what?' she said, doing the best she could to mimic Finn's voice. His lovely soft voice. 'I even took her to bed, but I didn't make love to her. No. I behaved so nobly—'

Her voice was cut off as he reached out and pulled her to him once more, his lips on hers, his hands wrenching the unzipped dress from her so that she lay completely naked in his arms. His fingers splayed across her cheek then moved down her throat, drawing thin skeins of heat across her shoulders, caressing her breasts. He bent his head to suckle them as he reached behind her, arching her body into his.

She had been daring him, goading him, taunting him for not responding to her, but she was totally unprepared for the overwhelming sensuality of his touch.

She knew she was crying, but somehow it didn't matter. All that mattered was Finn and the look in his eyes when he touched her. Nothing in her life had prepared her for this moment. And she knew quite simply that she had fallen absolutely and irrevocably in love with him.

And then, at the same instant, his hands stilled on her skin as he saw her tears. 'Is this so noble of me?' he asked angrily, and her heart shrivelled as she saw the way he was looking at her.

Turning from her abruptly, he got out of bed, grabbed his clothes and slammed out of the room.

Cara lay very slowly on the bed after he had gone. Surely it wasn't possible to feel this numb? She pulled the bedclothes to her chin and stared at the door. Perhaps Finn would never come back. No, that was silly. She picked at a loose thread on the coverlet. Even if the worse came to the worst, he had to come back, if nothing else for his things. Her eyes strayed to his grip and the slim briefcase next to it.

On an impulse she reached out and pulled it onto the bed, her hands smoothing over the glossy black leather. There was never going to be a better time to explore its secrets. And maybe, just maybe, it would let her in a little more on the feelings of the man who meant so much to her.

CHAPTER EIGHT

AN HOUR or so later Cara put the papers back in the case and stared unseeingly out the window. Then she got up, washed, dressed and brushed her hair with the care and impersonality of a well-trained robot. She had to find Finn. And when she found him she was going to get the truth.

He was downstairs in the low-beamed dining room. He had a tiny cup of coffee in front of him and he was staring at it as though it was the most interesting thing in the world.

She came to a halt by the table and looked at him, suddenly nervous. What would happen if he simply told her to go to hell?

He glanced at her and she sat down. Silence dragged between them. 'If I were a gentleman, I guess I would apologise for my behaviour up there,' he said at last. 'But considering my behaviour, I'm not a gentleman.'

She clenched her jaw. 'No, you're not,' she replied.

Finn looked at her as if shocked that she should be agreeing with him, then smiled. But the warmth didn't reach his eyes. 'That's what I like about you,' he remarked. 'You always tell the truth.'

She leant across to him. 'Unlike you,' she said.

His eyes narrowed. 'And what exactly do you mean by that?' he inquired.

'I mean—' she forced the words out, suddenly short of breath at the way he was looking at her '—that you know some sort of secret about my birth.'

135

He was absolutely still, watching her, saying nothing. 'I looked in your briefcase,' she said, the words tumbling out. 'I read every single cutting. And in half of them there are very strong hints that there was some cover-up, some mystery about my parents.' She swallowed. 'That they weren't really my parents after all.'

She stared straight into his eyes. 'That's why you came to my wedding, wasn't it?' she said. 'To find out if you could get something on it for a newspaper or even that new book of yours.'

He didn't move a muscle. 'No,' he said flatly. 'It wasn't. And you had no business poking about in my private papers.'

Cara sat back and stared at him. 'What about *my* private life?' she demanded.

He sighed. 'This is nothing to do with the newspapers,' he said at last. 'And that's all I'm going to say, so you can save your breath from questioning me.'

She lifted her chin. 'You never say anything,' she said bitterly. 'It's like travelling with the sphinx.'

Finn shrugged. 'It's better that way,' he drawled.

'For you, maybe,' Cara retorted. 'Not me.' She leant towards him again. 'Why haven't you told me any of this before? You could have told me something, at least.'

His forefinger traced the rim of the cup. 'No, I couldn't,' he replied. 'At first I didn't know whether I could trust you or not—you might have wanted to run back to Luca. I didn't know how you really felt about him, whether it was just nerves that made you want to duck out of the wedding, whether you really wanted to get away from him. And in any case,' he added, 'the less you know, the safer it is for all concerned.'

She thought of what had happened upstairs between them and her heart thudded. 'Is that why you didn't make love to me earlier?' she whispered. 'Because it's safer that way? Because you don't trust me?'

'No,' he said tersely. 'It's because I don't trust myself.'

'What do you know about my parents?' she demanded, unable to give up. 'I want you to tell me.'

He stared steadily at her. 'You'll find out when we get to England,' he said. 'And that's more than I was meant to tell you.'

The memory of the telephone call she had overheard him making in Monte Carlo came flooding back. She stared at him with absolute stillness. 'So you are working for someone else,' she whispered at last.

Holding her gaze, he nodded slowly. 'In a way,' he agreed.

'And you won't tell me?' she pleaded.

He shook his head. 'No. It's too dangerous.'

'Too dangerous for whom?' she asked bitterly. 'And since you're obviously protecting someone else, maybe even working for them, what does that make me, except a commodity again?'

Finn slammed his cup down in his saucer and glared at her. 'Do you really think I see you as some sort of object?' he demanded.

She nodded violently. 'Yes,' she retorted. 'And I've obviously got Not Wanted On Voyage written all over me.'

'If that's what you believe, that's fine by me,' he snapped. 'Frankly, I'm beginning to wish I'd never set eyes on you.'

She lifted her chin. 'Likewise,' she lied stiffly.

Finn leant across the table, put his hand on her shoulder and shook her. 'This is stupid,' he said. 'If we don't act together, I'll never get you away from Luca.'

'I don't care any more!' shouted Cara, Finn's words biting deep. Did he really wish he'd never met her?

His grip tightened on her shoulder. 'Yes, you do,' he said coldly.

It was no good. She could feel the fury and frustration snaking through her veins, and Finn's touch was all that was needed for her finally to explode. She banged her fist on the table, and Finn's cup danced in its saucer. 'For God's sake!' she yelled. 'It's my life! After all we've been through, you have to tell me!'

The only other person in the room, an elderly and slow moving waitress who had been coming across to them, stopped, turned swiftly on her heel and scuttled through the swing door to the kitchen.

'Careful, Cara,' Finn advised, his cool tones belying the dark passion of his eyes. 'At this rate neither of us will get any lunch.'

His calmness did more to upset her than anything else. 'I don't care about lunch,' she yelled. 'I want the truth!'

He leaned across the table once more and took her hand. 'You're going to have to wait,' he said. 'And considering the amount of questions you generally ask, I wish I hadn't even told you this much.'

She stared at him, trembling in spite of herself. There was nothing in the whole world she needed more at the moment than some simple human comfort. A few hours before, she might have been able to turn to Finn. Now that seemed impossible.

He looked at her consideringly. 'All that you've read in the cuttings is basically all I know,' he said at last. 'I didn't write those particular articles, I dug them out for extra background information about you. What rumours there were about you seemed to imply that you had been adopted as a baby. And even in the mind of the most mud-slinging reporter, that doesn't really mount up to scandal.'

Cara looked at her lap and twisted her fingers together. 'I'm sorry,' she said finally. 'It's just that...' She swallowed the lump in her throat. 'It's just that it's a bit of a shock to realise that the people I always thought of as my parents were no relation whatever.'

Finn looked at her a split second too long before replying, 'That's only a supposition in a newspaper, Cara. There's no need to take it as gospel.'

She gazed at him and shook her head. 'You wouldn't have those cuttings with you if you didn't think there was some truth in them. Would you?'

He said nothing to that, and she smiled bitterly at him. 'You won't tell me, will you?' she asked at last. 'And the only man who could is in hospital.'

There was sympathy in his eyes, concern, too, she realised with a shock, as she lifted her face to gaze at him fully. But there was another look, too, a secret, closed-in expression she couldn't interpret at all.

'What about your nanny, Sarah?' he asked abruptly, as if sensing her analysis.

She shook her head. 'She didn't come to live with us until I was about eighteen months old. And my uncle wouldn't tell anybody outside the family about a scandal.'

'What about you yourself, then?' he probed. 'There must be a lot of things you can remember about your childhood that would provide a clue as to who your parents were.'

Cara glared at him icily. 'Why should I tell you anything if you won't level with me?' she demanded.

He shrugged. 'Fair point, I suppose,' he conceded equably. 'Don't tell me, then. I don't suppose it really matters.'

Her eyes narrowed. There was something here she didn't understand at all. It was as if...as if he was playing with her. 'My childhood was perfectly normal,' she said. 'Boring, even.'

He raised an eyebrow. 'Is that normal as in just your average boring Mafia family?'

'You have no right to say these sort of things,' she snarled. 'My father was a good man. He was my uncle Pancrazio's brother.'

Finn looked her straight in the eye. 'Are you sure that's who your father was?' he drawled.

Cara opened her mouth and then closed it again. 'I came down here hoping you'd tell me those cuttings were all lies,' she whispered eventually. 'I couldn't believe it when I read them. I thought...I thought it was some cruel joke.' She took a cube of sugar and mindlessly unwrapped it and then wrapped it up again.

'My father—' She stopped. 'The man I have always thought was my father,' she amended. 'He had a motorcycle factory outside Turin. Not a big one,' she explained. 'Almost a one-man band, in fact. His motorcycles were fast, sought after, but—' She shrugged almost as if she couldn't go on.

'What happened?' Finn asked quietly.

'He took my...my mother for a ride on his latest one. Everyone tells me that he dreamt it was going to be the one to make his fortune. Their fortune,' she amended. 'It was a few months after I was born, I think. Not more than that.'

Finn looked at her gently. 'I read there was a crash, but there weren't too many details available. It was an awful thing to happen—I'm sorry.'

She nodded, unable to say more. She swallowed and looked at him pleadingly, 'Won't you tell me what you know? If I really am their child?'

'No,' he said, his face almost a mask. 'I can't.'

She sat utterly still, looking at his face, hoping against hope that he would relent, and then with a cry she leapt up from the table, ran out of the room and pounded up the stairs to their room.

She yanked open the big old-fashioned wardrobe and tearing out her clothes, stuffed them in the carriers Finn had originally given her.

'And just what do you think you are doing?' The hair lifted on the nape of her neck at the voice she knew so well, but she didn't turn around.

'What does it look like?' she snapped. 'I'm leaving.'

He was right behind her, she knew. But if anything it made her movements more frenzied. 'Cara,' said Finn softly, his hand coming round to rest on hers. 'Stop this.'

She whirled to face him. 'I'm going,' she yelled. 'And there is nothing you can do to stop me.'

'On the contrary,' he replied, his voice if anything even more calm. 'There are several things I can do.' He shrugged. 'I could lock you in the wardrobe and just trust to luck it isn't infested with killer woodworm.'

'Don't bother to try and get round me with that…with that—' He was too close, damn him. She pushed against him, but he didn't move.

'With that what?' he prompted.

'With that false charm of yours,' she snapped at last. 'You were right when you described yourself this morning, and I should have listened to you. You are worse than Luca. You pretend to be my friend and all the time you are working behind my back for your own ends.'

He gripped her arms. 'Listen to me, Cara,' he said urgently. 'Do you really think I want to hide things from you? Do you?'

She gazed into his eyes and wondered whether she could believe him. Whether she could trust him. It felt so natural to be with him, even when they shouted at each other. But who was this person looking out of that face she thought she had come to know so well?

He held her gaze, and after a moment she dropped her eyes. 'I don't know any more,' she whispered. 'All I know is that you are not who you say you are, and there are things, important things that you are not telling me. Is it so wrong of me to want to know what they are?'

He looked at her for a long moment and then folded her into his arms and held her tight. 'No, of course not,' he said at last, his face in her hair. 'But running away won't solve anything.'

'I'm not running away,' she snapped, her voice catching.

'Aren't you?' he inquired, drawing back from her. 'Where do you plan to go, exactly? And what are you going to use for money and transport?'

She shrugged and suddenly for some reason was unable to look him in the face. 'I was going to take the car,' she said as steadily as she could.

'Really?' he said coldly. 'And where does that leave me for transport?'

'You can get another hire car,' she burst out. 'Luca doesn't know your name. He's after me, not you.'

'And what makes you so sure of that?' Finn asked quietly. 'Considering Luca has some kind of paid contact in the police.' He sat on the bed and drew her down beside him. 'And,' he added silkily, 'how am I to know that you're not feeding him information yourself?'

'What?' she gasped.

'You heard,' he said calmly. 'Let's suppose you decided your only safe option was to go back to him. In that case it would make sense for you to tell him about me, as some sort of price of his forgiveness.'

'That's preposterous!' she shouted, half rising from the bed.

Finn's hand pulled her back. 'I agree,' he said softly. 'But you see the position I'm in. I have to be careful. I can't tell you all I know and I certainly can't let you run off.' He looked away for a moment, then back at her. The mockery had gone, but the expression in his eyes was still bleak. 'If Luca did happen to catch up with us...' he began, then stopped with a sigh.

'You just don't trust me, do you?' she asked bitterly.

'On the contrary,' he replied. 'I'd trust you with my life. But how much faith exactly do you have in me?'

He was sitting too close to her, so close her mind kept shooting off at nervous tangents. She didn't want to think about what he was saying. Didn't want to admit that he might be right. She moved slightly away and set her jaw. 'If you won't help me, Finn, and tell me all you know, then I warn you now, I'm going back to Naples. Only my uncle will know the answers to my questions. And I have to know who my parents are.'

He leant towards her until his face was close enough for a kiss. But the look in his eyes was anything but lover-like. She didn't think she had ever seen him so angry. She swallowed hard and lifted her chin.

'You are crazy,' he grated. 'One hundred per cent out to lunch. Do you really think that I am going to let you go back and put yourself in danger?'

'Why not?' she asked with a coolness she didn't feel.

He drew away slightly, his face tightening in exasperation. 'You know perfectly well why not,' he said.

'Well, it can't be because you care for me,' she retorted, tears suddenly too close to the surface. 'What happened here this morning proves that rather conclusively, don't you think?' She delved in her pocket for a hankie and didn't find one.

Finn watched her reach into another pocket, again with no success, and silently handed her a box of tissues from the bedside table.

'Thanks,' she muttered, blowing her nose. 'And whatever you might think,' she added fiercely, looking at him over the pastel-coloured tissue, 'I'd never betray anyone to Luca, no matter how—' She swallowed the lump in her throat and grabbed at the tissue box again. 'No matter how unreasonable and arrogant and selfish they are.'

His lips twitched. 'I do believe that's the nicest thing you've ever said to me,' he drawled.

She bunched the tissues up in her hand. 'Oh, go to hell!' she yelled, standing up and glaring at him. 'I wish I'd never met you! But I'm free now, and if I want to leave here, I shall. Whether you want me to or not.'

He scowled at her. 'In case you had forgotten,' he snarled, 'there's a maddened would-be bridegroom of yours breathing down our necks. If you do anything stupid, you won't get farther than the front gate, never mind Naples. We have to sit tight,' he added. 'Both of us. While we make contact with the police once more and find out what's going on. It's essential to know if they have discovered who the leak is and if they have found Luca.'

'You think they might have?' she asked hopefully.

He gazed at her steadily. 'It's possible,' he admitted. 'But I guess I don't hold out much hope at the moment. The car is hidden in Henri's barn, and we'll just have to trust to luck that Luca won't come here. And all that stuff about your parents,' he added impatiently. 'So far, it's just rumours and supposition. It's not worth risking your neck for.'

'It's my neck,' she flared. 'And my life.'

Silence fell between them. In the still heat of the afternoon she could hear strange scraping and creaking noises out in the yard, and then Henri and his wife arguing cheerfully with each other.

Finn had told her they had been married for years, and she thought with a pang of how content they seemed. Perhaps it was simply her fate to find herself with men who would never make her happy.

She bit her lip and sat on the bed again, suddenly feeling very weary.

'What's the matter?' he asked softly. 'If I didn't know you better, I'd think you were about to burst into tears.'

'Well, I'm not,' she replied unsteadily.

'Cara,' he asked. 'What is it?'

She swallowed and looked into his eyes. His blue, blue eyes. 'It's you,' she said reluctantly.

He held her gaze, but said nothing, merely reaching out to take her hand.

'You're only doing all this because you want a story, aren't you?' She sniffed. 'You were just...nice to me because you wanted something out of me, weren't you?' She twisted her hands together. 'And I fell for it,' she said bitterly. 'I made a complete fool of myself.'

'Cara.' He reached out and put his arm around her. 'That's not true, and you know it.'

She leapt away from him as though he had given her an electric shock. 'I don't know anything, remember?' she snarled, sitting as far down the bed as she could get. 'And it looks like I'm meant to stay that way. You could be anybody. I know nothing about you.'

He sighed. 'I tried to tell you only what you needed to know,' he said. 'At the start of all this, it seemed to me that our chances of escape were pretty slim. They're better now, but we're not home yet. And don't forget, Luca has his own reasons for disliking me, quite apart from me having helped you escape.'

'Because of that book you wrote about him.' She nodded slowly. 'I know. Except…' She shrugged. 'Except keeping me in the dark like this just makes me feel that you don't trust me at all. 'And that does make me wonder whether I can trust you. I mean,' she added, glancing at him, 'I suppose I know I can trust you, after all we've been through, but I don't *know* you, Finn. And I'd like to.'

'I'm not used to talking about myself,' he said, scowling at her. 'I'm generally the one asking the questions.'

She gazed steadily at him. 'But who are you, Finn?' she pressed. 'Really? Don't you think it would make me trust you more if I knew?' He was silent and she pressed home her argument.

'You seem to know pretty much everything about my background,' she went on as persuasively as she could. 'Why can't I know where you were born and what your parents were like? And Louise, the girl you mentioned this morning, who was she?'

She could see Finn's eye's darkening with impatience, and her torrent of questions slowed. 'I need to know about you.' She faltered. 'Surely you can see that?'

He sighed, and pulling a pillow behind him, leant back against the bed's headboard. 'My father was... is an industrialist,' he said coldly. 'And Louise was the only girl I've ever really fallen for. I was born in Boston, and my mother was Italian. She loved all things Irish—including my father—until she died, and named me after his ancestors. Cormac is my middle name. My surname is Bruton, but I dropped it after I left home.'

He folded his arms and looked at her. 'There. That satisfy you?'

She stared at him and bit her lip as she saw the hardness of his face. He had looked so different that morning when he held her in his arms. He had looked then as though he would give her everything in the world, down to the last piece of his soul. And she knew she had looked the same. How could they be so far apart now?

There was a choking sensation in her throat, and her eyes were stinging. Quickly she bent her head and traced with her finger the intricate pattern of the quilt.

His hand moved to cover hers, and she lifted her face to his at the unexpected contact. She gazed at him mutely, and his expression softened. 'My father is very wealthy,' he said quietly. 'And I was his only son. He had four daughters, but he's a very old-fashioned kind of guy, and I was seen as the heir to his fortune, the one who would work with him and eventually take over the business.'

Finn was looking at her as though he could see straight through her, as though he could see the events he was talking about.

'I guess you could say by the time I was twenty-one I was the biggest spoiled brat you could ever hope to meet,' he said flatly. 'I had money, quite a swanky car and there were plenty of girls who wanted me to take them places in it.'

He smiled bitterly. 'And then, you know what? I fell in love with a waitress in a coffee shop. She was truly...' Finn looked at Cara as if seeing her for the first time. 'Sweet, I guess. Corny word, but that's how Louise was. She wasn't exactly pretty, but—' He stopped for a moment, lost in the past, then shook his head. 'I don't know what it was. She just made me feel good, I suppose.'

Finn paused again and rubbed his forehead. 'Then the trouble really started,' he said. 'The daughter of my father's business partner came up to me one day and said she was pregnant and that I was the father. I couldn't believe it. Didn't want to believe it. I'd dated her for a while before I met Louise, and we'd taken precautions. But she stuck to her guns, and I accepted her word.

'Then before I knew what was happening, my father and her father had our wedding all mapped out. I didn't know what to do. I told Dad about Louise, but it was no use.' Finn stared expressionlessly at Cara. 'Wrong side of the tracks, you see. And then, of course, as he said, I had to face my responsibilities as a new father.

Louise would have to go, and I would have to marry Jane.'

He pressed his lips together and looked at his hands. 'Their arguments were pretty convincing. And I reckoned that in the circumstances they were right, so I did as they said. I went to see Louise, told her how it was, and when she started crying, God help me, I actually offered her money. Somehow, in some stupid way, I thought it would help. But all it did was make it worse.'

Finn paused and Cara held her breath, keeping her body as still as possible, afraid that the slightest movement would make him stop.

He looked at her and made a small helpless gesture with his hands. 'As the wedding got closer and closer,' he went on, 'I began to get this cold feeling in the pit of my stomach. But I stuck to the plans because I guess I had this naïve idea about family honour and all that.' Finn shot her a look. 'Seems like my father and your uncle have a great deal in common, doesn't it?'

She didn't answer, just let him hold her with his eyes, and he shrugged and went on. 'That all ended rather abruptly, though, on the morning of the big day, when I overheard the bride's mother gossiping and I discovered that my wife-to-be wasn't pregnant at all, that I had been tricked into the whole thing.'

There was silence. A quietness that seemed to stretch out into infinity. Even the strange noises in the yard below seemed to have become muted. 'What did you do?' asked Cara at last.

He looked directly at her, as if seeing her properly for the first time. 'What I should have done all along,' he replied grimly. 'I got straight in a car and drove to Louise's house like I was in the finals of the Indianapolis 500. I was going to apologise. Do anything I could to win her back. Offer her the moon, if necessary. Make her see that I really loved her, that we were both the victims of other people's ambitions. She would come round. I knew she would. I could see it all in my mind's eye.'

He glanced at Cara and fell silent.

'And?' she asked softly.

He looked at his hands as if he'd never seen them before. 'She'd taken an overdose the night before.' He gazed at her, and Cara felt her heart twist at the stark look in his eyes. 'She'd died a few hours later, in hospital.'

He sighed. 'And all along my family had just been manipulating me for their own ends, getting me married and settled down and dutifully groomed for the family business. The idea was suggested to Jane, I heard later, and she was only too willing to help. She was going to tell me after the wedding that the pregnancy was a false alarm, and by that time she reckoned I'd probably be hooked on her anyway.'

Finn smiled bitterly. 'A match made in heaven, my father called it. Plus it would stop me dreaming of some stupid career as a writer. All they had to do was feed me all this stuff about duty and honour, and it turned out I was young enough and stupid enough to believe them.'

He sighed. 'My father told me everything that night when I went home from the hospital. He shouted at me and slammed his fist on the desk and threatened to cut me out of his will because I'd run out on the wedding, but by then it didn't matter. I just didn't care any more. I got the truth out of him, packed my bags and left.'

Cara dropped her eyes from his face and concentrated once more on the pattern of the guilt. Not that she saw what she was staring at. But there was a look on Finn's face she simply couldn't bear to see.

She jumped when he reached out to tip up her chin. Almost unwillingly, she found herself meeting his eyes, knowing that Finn was looking straight into her soul. 'Do you think you know me any better now?' he asked with quiet grimness.

'Yes, I do,' replied Cara as steadily as she could. 'I know now why you stood up in that church for me.' She swallowed. 'Why you risked nearly everything to get me away.'

He nodded, his face shuttered. 'Maybe.'

She grasped his hand and leant towards him. 'You can't punish yourself like this,' she said. 'You can't, Finn. You were young and foolish, and your father and that girl you nearly married, they all manipulated you into doing something you certainly wouldn't have done on your own. It wasn't all your fault, and you have to forgive yourself.'

He stared at her stonily. 'If I wanted an analyst, I'd have gone to California,' he said angrily. 'I can manage just fine the way I am.'

'By closing yourself off?' she demanded.

He withdrew his hand and swung his feet to the floor. 'Wanting someone is not the same as loving them, Cara,' he said quietly. 'And I made a promise to myself a long time ago that I would never fall in love again.'

She shook her head. 'You can't do that to yourself,' she whispered, putting her hand on his.

She could feel his fist bunch underneath her fingers, as if he was physically stopping himself from taking the comfort she could give.

'What I do about my life is my business,' he said.

'Is it?' she asked softly.

'Do you know how many affairs I've had?' he demanded suddenly. 'Do you know how many women have sat as close to me as you're sitting now and called me all the names under the sun?'

She gazed at him mutely, and he shook his head. 'No. I thought not. And come to that, even I'd be hard put to give an exact number.'

'Is this some sort of macho mind game?' she asked, her heart thudding at his look. She was determined not to let him face her down.

He sat back and threw his hands in the air. 'I'm trying to tell you I'm no good for you,' he said.

Cara gazed at him. 'You saved me from marrying Luca,' she said.

'Maybe,' he said. 'But it was just because I was in the right place at the right time. You don't know me. I got you out of a tight spot, and you feel grateful. In a few weeks, when you've got to England, you'll have forgotten all about me. Which is as it should be.'

His lips twisted. 'It would be easy to love you, Cara,' he said softly. 'But I'm not going to. I'm going to get you to England and then I'm going to say goodbye. I'm not even going to get you to help me write that book of mine. So you're off the hook.'

'No!' she shouted, feeling as though suddenly she had to fight, to batter down the wall he had erected about his heart. 'You can't do this!'

'On the contrary,' he drawled. 'I can and I will.'

'But the way I feel for you,' she objected, her heart hammering at his stark tone. She swallowed the last remaining pieces of her pride. 'They are feelings I've never felt for anyone,' she whispered. 'I . . . I love you.'

'And who are you to tell me about love?' he asked with dangerous softness. 'What do you know about it? What do you really know about real life?'

He turned his head to stare at her, and she lifted her chin at the icy look in his eyes. 'More than you think,' she snapped.

'Oh, really,' he drawled. 'You must forgive me, I didn't realise I was pouring my heart out to a woman of such experience in these matters. 'Tell me,' he continued silkily. 'Exactly how many broken love affairs have you got through?'

CHAPTER NINE

CARA clasped her hands tightly, trying not to let herself be hurt at the way he was talking to her. 'I fell in love last year, if you really want to know,' she lied stiffly.

The look on his face would have been almost comical if only she hadn't been so angry at his goading. She glared at him. 'There's no need to look so surprised,' she snarled.

'Cara,' he said gently. 'You told me yourself this morning that you'd never slept with anyone before.'

Her lips parted. 'I lied,' she said abruptly.

'Really?' he drawled.

'Yes, really,' she replied. 'Do you think I've lived in a box all my life?'

'Yes,' he said simply. 'I can't imagine Luca letting any other man apart from your uncle get within three miles of you.'

'Well, you're wrong,' she snapped. 'I went to finishing school, you know.' She thought of the stark little chalet in the middle of nowhere and lifted her chin. 'For a year. In Switzerland.'

He leant towards her. 'I'm all agog,' he drawled, his tone loaded with mischief, but his eyes unable to hide his curiosity. 'Don't tell me. You seduced seventeen ski instructors and the man who came to wind the school clocks.'

She glared at him, then looked hurriedly away. 'You don't have to make fun of me,' she said bitterly. 'It didn't happen at the school, and I'm not going to tell you any more. You're just laughing at me.'

'Would I?' he drawled.

'Yes, you would,' she retorted. If she hadn't known him better she could have sworn that the hard lines on his face were softening to an expression of affection. But that was not possible. Not from Finn.

He lifted his hands placatingly. 'I'm not laughing at you,' he replied. 'Really. It's just...'

'Just what?' she demanded.

He looked at her again, and she could see that his eyes had softened to the colour of a dark summer sky. 'It's just that you have an amazingly pedestrian way of putting the most serious things.' He shrugged. 'You say you fell in love in the same way I imagine you'd announce you'd been on a sightseeing trip to Pompei.'

'And why not?' she demanded challengingly and then added, glaring at him, 'it was very educational. We didn't get out of bed once in three days.'

One of his eyebrows rose. 'Really?' he drawled. 'You must have been exhausted.' He leant towards her, and she stifled the urge to move away. 'Do tell me more,' he added coaxingly. 'I'm all ears.'

She glanced at him sharply. There was no mistaking the glint in his eye, but she couldn't back down now. She simply couldn't.

'He was very good-looking,' she answered at last. 'Much more handsome than you,' she added pointedly. 'And he wasn't at all arrogant, or infuriating, or... or bloody-minded, either.'

Finn's hand was stroking her arm, her pulse shuddering at his touch. 'Three days in bed, huh?' he murmured. 'Sounds quite a guy.'

'It was marvellous,' she affirmed. 'Do you want details?'

'No,' he drawled, his fingers sliding under the spaghetti straps of her thin dress. 'Maybe you can just show me, instead.'

She was trembling almost uncontrollably at his touch, but she had already moved to the very end of the bed. There was nowhere else to go. She jerked to her feet. 'Show you?' she asked, not wanting him to stop what he was doing but unable to ignore the sudden twanging of her nerves. 'What...what do you mean?'

He patted the bed. 'Oh, I'm sure a woman of experience like you knows exactly what I mean,' he drawled. 'Why don't you come here and we'll have an action replay?' She licked suddenly dry lips, but before she could say anything he swept on. 'I don't know that I can promise you three days, but—' he glanced at his watch '—how does twenty minutes sound?'

She took a step backward and cannoned into the wardrobe. This was not how she had pictured it at all. 'I...' she began and bit her lip.

'Cara,' he said softly.

'What?'

He shook his head. 'You're such a rotten liar,' he remarked at last. 'It's almost a shame to call your bluff.'

'I did meet someone,' she burst out. 'In Venice, if you really want to know! How dare you make fun of me!'

He reached out and took her hand. 'I apologise,' he said simply. 'You're right to be angry with me. But sometimes,' he admitted, 'I look at you and all sense seems to fly out the window.'

She stared at him for a long moment, unsure whether he was still making fun of her.

'Tell me about your affair,' he prompted, drawing her back to the bed.

'It wasn't an affair,' she said, reddening. 'I went to see some cousins in Venice while Luca and my uncle were away last summer, and one of them was very nice to me. That's all.' She stared dreamily at the wardrobe. 'Very nice.'

'Tell me,' he prompted.

There was a new note in his voice, a note that for some reason made her look at him again. He couldn't possibly be jealous. Could he? She searched his face for some clue as to his feelings, but there wasn't one.

'We drank champagne in the Piazza San Marco,' she said carefully. 'And then he took me home in a gondola and kissed me in the moonlight.' She sighed wistfully as she remembered how completely empty it had all been. As if Giulio had been reading from some manual.

Finn reached for her hand, his face if anything even more expressionless. 'And did he tell you how beautiful you were?' he remarked.

'Yes,' she said, remembering. 'All the time, and without any meaning whatsoever. It was almost as though he was scared to touch me. As if,' she added, 'he was constantly looking over his shoulder.'

Finn nodded as if that didn't surprise him in the least, but his face remained perfectly serious. 'Do you want to see him again?' he inquired.

'No.' She shook her head. 'All he could talk about was whether my uncle would give him a job. He would have been very boring as a long-term lover.'

She stared into Finn's face. 'You're laughing at me again,' she accused, her heart banging nervously.

He nodded, then shook his head rapidly. 'Yes...I mean no,' he amended. He smiled. 'I can't help it, Cara. I'm not making fun of you, it's just that the things you say have that effect on me sometimes.' His face straightened at the look in her eyes. 'And Luca,' he went on smoothly. 'He fitted the bill, then, of long-term love?'

She stared at him in surprise. 'He wanted to marry me, not love me,' she said simply. 'I suppose I agreed because it represented freedom. But by the time it got to the wedding I had realised I was just exchanging my uncle's set of rules for Luca's. And the more I thought about it, the more I couldn't go through with it.'

The strange noises in the yard had got louder now, creakings and bangings, and their eyes strayed to the window. Swearing under his breath, Finn got up and strode to it.

'What's happening?' asked Cara, following him.

Together they leant over the window sill, gazing at a scene of organised chaos. 'They're putting up trestle tables, like they're going to celebrate something,' replied Finn. Leaning out, he shouted a question at Marie, directing operations while her husband wandered about in the shade stacking wine bottles on a table that had already been erected.

Marie beamed up at them and unleashed a torrent of French that went straight over Cara.

'Well?' she demanded when Marie at last stopped. 'What's happening?'

Finn turned to her with an absolute poker face. 'They're putting on a party to celebrate our wedding,' he replied.

Cara stared hard at him. 'Is this some sort of a trick?' she demanded.

Finn shook his head. 'No,' he answered.

That single word seemed to have a finality about it that brought back everything he had said to her that morning. And his expressionless tone struck a chill into her heart. He would never love her, and she had been a fool to think he might. He just thought of her as an awkward parcel he had to deliver to England.

She stepped away from him and lifted her chin. 'You needn't worry,' she said coldly. 'I'll go and tell Marie somehow that it's all been a big misunderstanding.'

His hand caught her arm and turned her to him. 'Don't be ridiculous,' he snapped. 'What do you think you are going to tell her?'

She lifted her head and stared straight at him. 'The truth, of course,' she replied. 'What else?'

'The truth?' he echoed sceptically.

'Yes,' she snapped, her voice unreasonably quavery. 'That we are a completely mismatched couple and it's all been a big mistake.' She glanced at him. 'I read in a magazine once that some people have actually split up before their reception's even over. So our few days together should make us seem quite a long-term couple.' She shrugged, trying to sound light-hearted. 'Although it's not quite in the thirty-year class of Marie and Henri, I suppose.'

His grip on her arm tightened. 'You're hurting me,' she said unsteadily. 'You better let me go, and then I can arrange to get a separate room, as well.'

But instead of letting her go, he was pulling her closer, until she was in his arms and he was kissing her as if he never wanted to stop.

It was not until the scattering of laughter and applause from onlookers in the yard had stopped that Finn's grip loosened and he stared at her with a look she couldn't read at all. 'If they want to give us a party,' he said grimly, 'then we'll damn well accept.'

Cara pulled away from him, the blood thundering in her ears. How dare he treat her like this! 'Don't think I'm going,' she snapped. 'Because I'm not.'

Finn glared at her. 'You are going,' he snarled. 'If I have to put you over my shoulder and carry you. And you will look as though you are enjoying yourself.'

She lifted her chin. 'You are just as bad as Luca,' she retorted. 'Scratch the surface and there you are—a cave-man.' She wrenched her hand away furiously and stalked to the other side of the bed. As a barrier between them it was worse than useless, but she was not going to turn and flee. 'Do you really think you can order me around?'

There was a look in his eyes that made her want to breathe deep to control the way she was trembling.

'I'm not Luca,' he snapped. 'And you damn well know it. But you should also have the sense to realise, without me telling you that we have to appear to be together.'

She stared at him silently, and he turned abruptly so that he was once more looking out the window, staring unseeingly at the long trestle tables in the yard below.

'We simply have no choice but to go along with their plans,' he said harshly. 'We can't afford to start any speculation that we are not a happily married couple. I'd rather Marie and Henri had never started this, but now they have, we can't back down.'

Slowly she bent and picked up her clothes from the floor. She knew he was walking towards her, standing over her, knew without looking the kind of look he had on his face.

Straightening, she clutched the bundle of clothes to her as if they were some kind of protection. But against what, she couldn't have said.

'I said I was sorry for putting you through this, Cara,' he said more gently. 'And I mean it. You've been really brave all through this trip. I went to that church with a lot of misconceptions about you, but I really admire the way you stood up to Luca and the way you've dealt with everything since.'

Cara swallowed hard. Insults would have been easier to bear than this. It was almost more than she could do to stop herself from reaching up and touching his face, wanting him with such an ache deep inside that it was pure torture to step back and look away. 'I'll go and see if Marie needs any help,' she said a little wildly, turning for the door. 'There's still several hours before we need to get ready.'

Marie was only too pleased to see her, but refused to let her help in any way. She could speak no Italian, but knew more than a smattering of English. Before Cara knew what was happening she found herself being led to a couple of chairs in the shade and sitting down with Marie.

The older woman poured them both a glass of wine and then raised it to Cara. 'Good health,' she proclaimed and then looked seriously at her. 'You look unhappy. Is everything between you and Finn all right?'

Cara's jaw must have dropped because she suddenly realised that Marie was smiling at her and shaking her head. 'Forgive me, I am just a nosy old woman. But Finn is very dear to me. And I was so happy to see him married at last.'

Cara opened her mouth to speak and closed it again. She didn't have the words to explain what was happening nor, when she saw the kindness on Marie's face, the willpower. This was something she and Finn were going to have to work out on their own.

'Everything's fine,' she said as lightly as she could. 'It's just...we've been travelling a lot.' She gestured helplessly. 'Finn's got a lot on his mind at the moment.'

Marie topped up her glass and smiled conspiratorially at her. 'It is good to see him married. There are times, I admit, when I thought he would always be alone. And that is not good for a man like him.'

'No?' asked Cara, surprised at this new picture of Finn.

Marie glanced at her oddly. 'But surely you must agree, *chérie*, considering you are now married to him?'

Cara tried to pull her scattered wits together. 'I mean,' she said hurriedly, 'it was a whirlwind romance. I have to admit I don't know much about how Finn used to be.'

'Closed up,' Marie replied simply. 'Like an empty house.' She smiled at Cara. 'But you have changed all that, even in such a short time.'

'I have?' asked Cara.

Marie nodded. 'I said to Henri last night, there is a look in Finn's face when he gazes at that girl that I have not seen before. Take my word for it, Henri, I said, that is a marriage that will be very happy.'

She patted Cara's hand and got to her feet. 'I must go,' she said. 'There is a lot to do if we are going to celebrate successfully tonight. But you stay here and relax,' she urged. 'You don't need to help.'

Cara took Marie at her word. Somehow it seemed safer to stay in her chair than to risk another row with Finn. The tension between them was almost unbearable, and she didn't know how to handle it. Then as the shadows began to lengthen over the cobbled yard, she got up with a sigh and went inside the *auberge*.

Finn wasn't in their bedroom, and after selecting her clothes for the evening, she trudged dispiritedly along to the bathroom.

She was beginning to think that the strain of pretending to be married to him was far greater than the constant knowledge that Luca was even now looking for them and could even now be at the gate. On impulse she glanced out the window, but there was nothing there. Nothing except a few people beginning to arrive for a party it would take all her courage to attend.

She gazed dispiritedly at her reflection in the bathroom mirror and scowled at her feebleness. To her intense surprise, the expression gave her a sudden similarity to her uncle. And it was a look he wore that would make even Luca back down.

This was no time to give in, she thought with a sudden rush of stubborn anger. Finn was the man she wanted. The only man she could love. And if he wanted a wife for tonight, then he was damn well going to get one. There were more ways than one to melt an iceman.

Marie had agreed to lend her make-up and a hair-drier, and after bathing and washing her hair, she stalked along to the older woman's room to change. If Finn wanted to know where she was, he could just stew.

At last she was ready. Her hair loose and wearing the prettiest dress she could find in the carriers Finn had given her, she returned to their room, her head up, her eyes blazing.

She put her hand on the doorknob and stood for a moment, fighting to keep her sudden surge of feelings under control. But before she could turn it, the door was yanked open and Finn stood there, furious.

'Where the hell—' he started, then stopped.

'Yes?' she said politely, unable to stop the way her heart leapt at the expression on his face, then added as coolly as she could, 'was there something?'

'That dress,' he began.

She looked at it and smoothed an imaginary crease. 'You bought it for me,' she said softly.

He reached out and tipped up her chin with his hand. 'You've done something to your eyes,' he added. 'And your hair. It's—'

'Been washed,' she supplied in as practical a tone as she could manage, wishing her pulse wouldn't behave quite so erratically every time he touched her. 'I...' She stopped and made an effort to keep her voice as light as possible. 'I thought I might as well look as though I actually care for you.'

He stepped out of the room and took her arm, his fingers warm on her skin, his touch doing nothing to calm her suddenly bouncing heart rate. 'Good idea,' he drawled with a look in his eyes that told her he knew exactly what a turmoil she was in.

'I can walk perfectly well unaided,' she snapped as he closed the door, still holding her. That wasn't what she had meant to say at all, she thought, mentally kicking herself. But Finn's closeness, the way he looked and smiled at her, were unsettling to say the least.

'Have you seen the state of the stair carpet?' he asked conversationally, propelling her along the landing. 'Shocking. Really. I mean, without me to hold onto, you'd probably fall down the stairs and do serious injury to all the guests at the bottom.'

'I'd like to push you down the stairs,' she retorted, all ideas of cool diplomacy evaporating rapidly.

He grinned at her suddenly. 'This must be what it's like to be really married, don't you think? All these fireworks. Maybe we should try it for real sometime.'

With a cry she wrenched her hand away and stepped back, glaring at him. 'How dare you say that to me?' she yelled. 'How dare you?'

He stepped towards her, his face concerned. 'Cara,' he said reasonably. 'It was a joke.'

'Not a very funny one,' she snapped, very close to tears.

He tipped up her chin with his hand and looked right into her eyes. 'What?' he asked softly. 'What's the matter?'

Cara swallowed and gazed at him, unable to keep up the pretence any longer. 'You really don't believe how much I love you, do you?' she asked simply.

His face took on that still, watchful look that she hated so much.

She shook her head. 'I thought I could play along with you tonight, could put on a show and maybe...' She faltered. 'Maybe even dazzle you a little. But—' She shook her head again. 'I can't do this, Finn.'

He had obviously just had a shower, and there was a bead of water trickling down his cheek. Without thinking she reached up and smudged it away. His hand came up and enclosed her fingers. They gazed at each other for a moment, then Finn turned abruptly from her.

'You look very beautiful tonight,' he said.

'So do you,' she replied, flustered, clenching her fingers.

He turned to face her once more, as if undecided about something, then took her hand and looked into her troubled eyes. 'It doesn't matter what you say, Cara,' he said. 'I don't love you.'

She swallowed and looked away, tears pricking her eyelids. 'I know.'

There was a muscle thudding in his jaw, and he reached out, gently turning her face to his. 'There is one advantage in all this,' he said grimly.

She looked at him questioningly and he went on. 'It will be one sure-fire way to get rid of that ridiculous fantasy of yours that you love me.'

'I don't know what you mean,' she said.

'Oh, I think you do,' he drawled, his voice and face once more absolutely deadpan. 'This evening is going to give me ample opportunity to treat you like you've always wanted to be treated. I'll kiss you and hold your hand and tell everyone how much I love you. What could be wrong with that?'

'Because it's a lie,' she whispered, an awful feeling suddenly worming its way into the pit of her stomach.

He nodded slowly. 'Exactly,' he said softly. 'And maybe by the end of the evening you'll realise how much of a lie, an illusion, you're living at the moment. And that you don't really love me at all.'

'You're not being fair,' she responded. 'You know you're not.'

'All's fair in love and war,' he said flatly. 'And you have to realise that this is not love. You can't know what love is, Cara. You're too young, and I'm completely the wrong man for you.'

'Are you?' she asked. 'How can you tell?'

'When Luca asked you to marry him,' Finn went on inexorably, 'you said yes because you built this great huge fantasy about what life would be like once you were Signora Finzi. Now you're building a fantasy about me. Let's see how you can cope with it in practice.'

It was almost as though her heart had stopped. But she lifted her chin and looked him straight in the eye. Only bleakness stared back at her.

'Play your game, Finn, and have your laugh at my expense,' she said, dragging her hands from his. 'Believe that I don't love you, if it makes you feel better.'

She swallowed hard. 'I fantasised about the life I would have with Luca, not about him.' Her eyes strayed down, then up once more. 'I know how I feel about you, and I can't help it. And nothing you can say or do will alter that fact. I love you.'

He stared steadily at her, a muscle jumping in his cheek, and then putting his hand under her elbow he escorted her downstairs to the party.

The food was magnificent, but it almost choked Cara to eat it. Marie and Henri kept smiling at her, gesturing that she should eat more, that she was too pale, but there was no way she could explain anything nearing the truth to them.

She and Finn had been given the place of honour at the top of a long trestle table covered with a starched white cloth. People from the nearby village who had known Finn for years kissed him and her as they arrived in the lantern-strung yard and pressed little presents into their hands.

It was almost more than she could bear. She looked at the little pile in front of her, a jar of prunes in eau de vie, another of foie gras, a square of traditional French linen, and felt the tears prick her eyelids.

'You okay?' asked Finn quietly.

'No,' she replied, momentarily off balance from the sincere note of his voice. To have Finn sitting next to her in the place of honour, smiling at her, holding her hand, kissing her cheek and piling her plate with things to eat was turning into pure torture. Because he was putting it all on.

'Stop it,' she whispered wretchedly, glancing at him and then looking away.

'But this is reality, Cara,' he replied in a harsh undertone. 'This is what it would be like if we were really married. And now you know that you don't like it.'

She threw her fork onto her plate and glared at him. 'Of course it's not reality,' she shouted. 'You're the one who lives in a fantasy world,' she added. 'You think you can just shut love out, snap your fingers and make it go away. But it doesn't work like that.' She paused and shook her head. 'Even I can tell you that.'

There was an expression in his eyes that told her she'd struck home, and she swept on. 'Do you think I want to fall in love with an image?' she demanded. 'Do you really think I am as silly and inexperienced as that?'

'What do you want?' he asked gently, his face expressionless, but for the merest fraction of a second, before the shutters came down, his eyes had been softer than she had ever seen them.

Her heart leapt and then fell. 'I want you,' she whispered. She looked at him. 'I don't know why I fell in love with you,' she said in a rush, her words tumbling out almost on top of each other. 'Sometimes I would give almost anything not to care about you. But I can't. It's just not something I can do anything about.'

Cara shrugged helplessly. She might as well say all the things in her heart. It was doubtful that she would ever get another chance, she thought with a pang, because in another few days, when she got to England, she might never see Finn again.

'I suppose if I were to analyse it,' she continued, 'it's the way you look at me...the way you touch me.'

People were looking up the table at them, but she was past caring if anyone could hear what she was saying. What she had to say was too important. 'The way you make me laugh,' she added, holding his eyes with hers, hoping against hope that they would soften again at her words.

'And...you think about me,' she went on. 'You bought me those espadrilles in the service station, and those clothes in Monte Carlo. You were prepared to give up the whole bed for me to sleep in here, even when you were so tired that you fell asleep where you sat.'

But Finn's face didn't change, and she trailed off. 'I'm sorry,' she mumbled. 'Since you don't love me, this is all probably highly embarrassing for you.' It was best not to look at him, she thought. Those eyes of his were altogether too unsettling.

She steeled herself for one last shot. 'I'd rather have you as a friend, Finn, than undergo this kind of torture, this—this false love,' she said. 'I think the way you are acting stinks.'

His eyes were almost black in the dim light, and he looked the picture of ease except for his fist clenched tight on the tablecloth. 'I don't care what you think,' he said in clipped, harsh tones.

Her head snapped back. 'Damn you, Finn Cormac,' she said in a snarling whisper. 'Damn you to the depths of hell for this!'

He smiled at her, but the warmth didn't reach his eyes. 'So much for soft words,' he said with a weariness that struck right to her heart. 'I'm sorry, Cara, but you had to see for yourself that it's just not going to work.'

'Don't you have feelings at all?' she pleaded.

There was that expression again in his eyes as he looked at her that gave her a sudden leaping hope, but then he looked away, his fingers dropping, and the moment died. 'No,' he replied. 'I don't.'

'Maybe you have a reason for doing this to me,' she said. 'But how can you lie to your friends like this? How can you?'

'Because, in case you've forgotten,' Finn drawled, flashing a brilliant false smile at some people down the table, 'our lives could be in danger. If Luca is anywhere near here, which I was told earlier on the phone that he must be, even he could put two and two together if he suddenly heard gossip about an American and an Italian girl who were supposed to be married and then turned out not to be.'

She glared at him. 'I'm beginning to think marrying Luca might have been a far more peaceful option than running away with you.'

'See,' he said, 'I told you my strategy would work.'

Her lips tightened. 'How about this for a strategy, then,' she said, smiling brightly at him and knocking his wineglass into his lap.

Without even missing a beat he took her hand, kissed it, then pressed it flat into her plate of gateau. 'Darling,' he drawled. 'How clumsy of you.' Carefully he picked up her hand and placed it on her knee, pressing her fingers gently into the thin cotton of her dress.

Then he stood, joined in the easy banter about his wine-stained trousers, kissed Cara on the cheek and went to change his clothes.

Cara sat, outwardly laughing and nodding at the pantomimed remarks of her neighbours, and inwardly seething at what Finn had done. That last kiss he planted on her cheek felt as though it was burning a hole in her skin.

Just wait till he comes back, that's all, she thought. She would kick him right where it hurt. *Let him explain that as a lovers' quarrel, if he wanted to, and damn the consequences.*

And then the heat of her sudden anger died, leaving only a cold ache behind. Finn didn't love her, and she had fallen irrevocably for him. It was an impossible situation. And what did he expect to do when it was time to go to bed? Her heart thudded at the idea of how she would like it to turn out, but it was no use. He wanted her, but he didn't love her. At least he had tried to be honest.

Pushing back her chair, she smiled at the others and got up. She would take a walk. She desperately needed to think.

But as she turned from the table she saw Finn coming towards her. And he was not alone. Cara's heart stilled as she saw that the man beside him was Luca.

She stood perfectly straight, watching them come closer and closer across the yard, the cobbles splashed with yellow from the lamps.

Finn's face was set, expressionless, but Luca, Luca, she thought with a shaft of fear, had that look on his face that she had seen before. The look that meant he was just about to erupt in rage.

Luca was right in front of her, as close as he had been to her in front of the altar. Cara gripped her chair and steeled herself not to back away.

CHAPTER TEN

CARA gazed into Luca's face and wondered how she could ever have agreed to marry him. It was as if he was a near-stranger she had met a long time ago, and not the man she had stood next to at the altar only a few days before.

She found herself looking at him as if she had never seen him before, noting the obvious expense of his clothes, the sheen on his dark silk weave suit, the big signet ring and chunky gold cuff-links, the crocodile shoes. Everything he wore, down to his overwhelming aftershave, shouted money, money, money.

He was running to fat, too, and his skin looked sallow and unhealthy in the lamplight. It was impossible not to compare him to Finn, impossible not to shiver at what she had so nearly done. To shiver at what might happen now.

All talking around the table had stopped, and everyone was staring at them. Henri had a fork poised in mid-air before his half-opened mouth.

Luca stared from Finn to Cara and back again. 'You are both coming with me,' he ordered. His right hand had not once come out of his pocket, and Cara knew, without even thinking about it, that he was holding a gun.

And then, glancing once more at Finn, Luca added, 'Tell these people some plausible story as to why we are leaving. I can speak French, so don't try any tricks. If they call the police I will kill you both.'

Finn looked as though he was having a conversation about the weather, Cara thought. But there was a look in his eye she had never seen before. 'Tell them yourself,' he said at last. 'I'm not your personal messenger.'

For one awful second Cara thought Luca was going to hit Finn, or worse. And she knew Luca too well to misread how enraged he was. But after a second he turned to Henri and spoke to him in halting French.

'Now,' he snapped, turning back to them. 'You will both come with me.'

Cara's heart seemed to leap and fall and then keep on falling at the seeming inevitability of what was happening. They were trapped, and this time there was no way out.

It was like watching a slow-motion film with the sound turned off, she thought wretchedly, as they walked around the corner of the *auberge*, cutting themselves off from the view of the table.

Then, amazed, she saw Finn turning and stopping by Henri's piled-up crates of empty wine bottles, putting his body between her and Luca.

'Take me,' he said quietly. 'You don't need Cara.'

'I'll take both of you,' snapped Luca. 'Now get going.'

Finn didn't budge. 'Did you really think,' he asked reasonably, 'that we would stay here without a police bodyguard?'

Luca's gaze flickered around the surrounding buildings, and Finn pressed home his advantage. 'If you try anything there are officers all around who have orders to shoot. Take me with you as a hostage and you might have a chance.'

'No, Finn,' said Cara urgently. 'You can't do this.'

'She was promised to me,' retorted Luca. 'And I will make her honour that, if it's the last thing she does.

Who are you to tell me what I should and shouldn't do?'

'She's nothing to you,' said Finn steadily. 'And you've already told me you know who I am.'

Luca nodded slowly. 'Don't worry,' he said. 'I intend to make you pay for every lie you wrote about me.'

Finn took a step towards him. 'So take me and you will be seen to have your revenge,' he argued. 'Both for the book and for taking Cara away. Leave her. What will marrying her do for you now? Especially now that Pancrazio Gambini is dead?'

Cara drew her breath in sharply at the news but read instantly in Finn's glance that he wanted her to say nothing.

Luca gazed from one to the other of them, his gaze resting finally on Finn. 'Why did you take her?' he asked. 'Were you paid?'

Finn stared at him for a long moment. 'Yes,' he said at last, his voice flat, expressionless. 'I was paid.'

Luca looked at him closely, then stepped back, shaking his head. 'Don't lie to me, Cormac. You love her, don't you?' he demanded, and as Cara stared at Finn she forgot to breathe.

'Don't you?' pressed Luca.

'Yes, I love her,' said Finn. He stared straight into Luca's eyes. 'And if you harm her in any way I'll kill you.'

Luca nodded, then smiled as if at a secret joke. 'You are not exactly in a position to bargain with me,' he drawled. 'But I think you have just made yourself a deal, Mr. Cormac.'

Shooting a glance at Cara, his smile widened. 'You are free to go.'

Cara stared at him numbly. 'I don't understand,' she said.

Luca shrugged. 'It's really very simple. Your uncle is dead, so I no longer need you. Mariella—'

'Your mistress?' broke in Cara, astonished. 'What's she got to do with this?'

He nodded. 'My mistress, as you so quaintly put it, will be pleased because she has this foolish notion that I am now going to marry her.' He shrugged. 'It also means I won't have any trouble with whatever relations of yours, Cara, might decide to start a blood feud just because I've got rid of you. And—' he sighed with satisfaction '—it will be good to take this man back,' he added, nodding at Finn. 'It will show how I exact my revenge.'

'But I will be free,' said Cara, a little wildly. 'How will you get pleasure out of that?'

For one brief second Luca smiled, then looked at her with an expression that made her feel cold. 'Quite simply,' he replied. 'You have no money, no home, no friends. The thought gives me great pleasure. You shamed me by running off with Cormac. Now you can spend all your life wondering what I did to him. And you will never know.' With a jerk of his head, he motioned to Finn to start walking.

It was as though she was a spectator to the whole event, numbly watching something that she couldn't believe. But Luca's sudden movement galvanised Cara into action. 'You can't do this!' she screamed, lunging after them and grabbing Luca's arm.

Without the least effort he shook her off, and she stumbled then straightened, her chin up.

'Please don't do this,' she whispered.

'Why should you worry?' Luca demanded. 'You are free to go. I do not care what happens to you.'

Cara gripped her dress with both hands and stared at him. There was a large grease spot on the skirt where Finn had put her cake-covered hand. It was ridiculous to think that that had happened less than half an hour ago.

'Please,' she offered wildly. 'I'll do anything. I'll go back with you. Marry me. Do anything you say. But don't do this. Don't take Finn away.'

Luca gazed at her speculatively, and Finn turned to look at her. 'Go on, Cara,' he ordered, his rough tones belying the tenderness in his eyes. 'Get out of here.'

'No,' she shouted. 'You can't do this to save me. I won't let you.'

Luca stepped towards her, watching both of them. 'So,' he said conversationally. 'You offer to marry me at last. I should be honoured.'

She ignored the warning signals beginning to flash in her brain and reached out to him. 'Will you let him go if I come back with you?' she pleaded.

Finn made an impatient gesture with his hands. 'Don't be ridiculous,' he said harshly. 'Get away from here before you get hurt.'

She clenched her jaw. 'I don't care,' she said, and then she swallowed hard at the expression in his eyes and wrenched her gaze away, turning once more to Luca. His eyes were small, watchful, and her heart quailed. But she had at least to try to save Finn. Even if she had to say things she had never imagined she would utter.

Cara gazed pleadingly at Luca. 'You can't know how sorry I am for what I have done to you,' she began again. 'Truly,' she went on hurriedly, seeing the expression on Luca's face. 'You've always been so important in my life. That day of our wedding was just so...over-whelming. It was all arranged so fast. I...I just couldn't cope.'

'You seemed to cope quite well with running away,' said Luca. It was strange how calm he was acting, when she could physically feel the rage inside him.

'No.' She shook her head uncertainly. 'It was all so unreal—just like a game, I suppose. But I missed you as soon as we left.'

She lifted her chin and stared him straight in the eye. 'But I was too frightened to come back to you, to ask you to forgive me.'

Luca stared at her for a long moment. 'You hurt me very much by running away like that,' he said at last. It was as if the mask had dropped, and for a second she could see a glimpse of the Luca she had known as a boy. His voice as wistful as it was that day long ago when his pet dog was killed and she had comforted him.

'Please, Luca,' she whispered. 'Let him go. He means nothing to either of us now we are back together. He was just in it for the money. I deliberately didn't tell him who you were, otherwise I know he wouldn't have helped me.'

She licked her lips nervously and stared once more at her former bridegroom. 'I will come back with you and be your wife. Do anything you say. I know now how wrong I was, and I bitterly regret hurting you.'

But the brief moment of closeness had gone. It was Luca the man standing in front of her, staring at her with barely concealed contempt. 'You have dishonoured me in front of my whole family,' he said at last. 'You are nothing to me.'

It was useless. Useless to even hope that she could fool him. Anger and frustration overwhelmed her. 'I never was anything to you,' she said bitterly. 'You wanted to marry me simply to cement good relations with my uncle.'

Out of the corner of her eye she could see Finn moving as delicately as a cat up on Luca's blind side. She glared at her former bridegroom, suddenly hoping that somehow she could distract him long enough to help Finn. 'And you had a mistress,' she swept on. 'I was nothing to you but a piece of property.'

Luca's face darkened. 'Maybe,' he snapped. 'But you were mine.'

Cara clenched her fists and stared him right in the eye. Unbidden, conversations she had had with Finn came floating into her mind. 'I don't believe I'm having this conversation with a man in the twentieth century,' she said. 'You are such a macho bully you should be stuffed and put in a museum.'

Luca couldn't have looked more surprised if she had struck him. She flashed a glance at Finn, and her heart lifted unreasonably when she saw he was almost behind Luca.

'Go, Cara,' grated Luca. 'Or I will shoot you both now and damn the consequences.'

She swallowed. 'You wouldn't dare,' she sneered, wondering exactly how far she could push him before he went right over the edge.

He stepped towards her, putting himself directly between her and Finn. 'I don't give a damn about you any more,' Luca snarled. 'In a way you benefited me a great deal by running out of the church that day.'

'I did?' Cara asked, instinctively stepping back, realising too late that she was drawing him farther from Finn.

'You were right,' he snarled. 'It was merely good politics that made me decide to marry you, but now I don't need you any more.'

Luca stepped closer to her. 'In fact,' he said with chilling smoothness, 'to have anything to do with you now that your uncle is dead might be seen as a bit of a liability.'

Cara's eyes snapped with anger, and she forgot momentarily about the extreme danger she was in. 'How dare you say such a thing about a man who was always so kind to you,' she snapped. 'He treated you like a son.'

Luca reached across and clamped her face in his fingers. 'And why not?' he demanded. 'Considering I was marrying his daughter?'

Cara's eyes widened, and Luca stared into her face. 'Can you honestly say you didn't know he was your father?' he asked.

She breathed in sharply, and he dropped his hand. 'I see not,' he said. 'But it doesn't matter. He is dead, and I don't need you any more. But by God, I will have my revenge on this man.'

'What man?' inquired Finn quietly. And as Luca turned, he hit him very neatly over the head with a wine bottle.

Cara looked at the man at her feet, then at Finn. The bottle dropped out of his hand, and he reached out for her, pulling her into his arms, his hand stroking through her hair, holding her so tight she thought she'd never breathe again.

'Are you all right?' he asked.

'Yes,' she whispered, her mind still reeling at what had just happened.

He pulled back a little and looked at her with an expression she had never seen before.

'You...you really do...care about me, don't you?' she asked in astonished disbelief.

For one split second he looked at her totally expressionlessly, and her heart thudded.

'Care about you?' he echoed in amazement.

'Don't you?' she faltered.

Finn's hand cupped her cheek, his thumb stroking her skin. 'Cara, I love you more than I can say. You don't know how much I've...' He trailed off, staring into her eyes. 'Oh, hell,' he muttered. 'This is how I feel about you,' and leaning down he kissed her as though he never wanted to stop.

It seemed several years before they stopped, Finn pulling away with the utmost reluctance as the rest of the guests came pounding around the corner of the barn to see exactly what was going on.

It was later, much later, that they had a proper chance to talk. After the police had been and taken Luca away under heavy guard, and after all the guests had been smoothed down with more wine, happily gossiping over the evening's amazing events as they wandered unsteadily away in the velvet darkness.

Cara leaned against the window of the little room it seemed she and Finn had shared for a lifetime, then glanced at the man who had come to mean so much to her.

'I just can't believe my uncle's dead,' she muttered at last. 'I keep thinking about it, and I can't feel sad because I can't believe it.' She glanced at Finn. 'Why are you looking at me like that?' she asked. 'You've got that expression on your face that means you know something I don't.'

Finn shrugged. 'I lied about your uncle,' he said at last.

'You what?'

'I did it to force Luca's hand,' he explained.

'Well, thank you for telling me afterwards,' she said.

'If you remember rightly,' he drawled, 'I was concentrating on something else at the time. You.'

She tried to glare at him and failed miserably. 'He's really all right?' she asked, tension draining out of her body as Finn nodded.

He was looking at her in that way that made her want to go to him, to kiss him, to feel his arms around her again. But she had one more question.

'Is it true?' she asked softly. 'About...about the other thing?'

He gazed at her for a moment. 'That I love you?' he replied.

She smiled and shook her head. 'No, I mean, is my uncle really my father?'

Finn nodded. 'Yes, it's true.'

'And my mother?' she asked.

Finn crossed the room to stand in front of her. 'I think you know the answer to that one,' he said quietly.

'It's Sarah, isn't it?' she asked.

Finn nodded. 'I met her when I was researching that book about Luca, and when she heard you were getting married to him, she rang me and asked if I would go, to find out somehow if you were happy, if there was anything that you needed.'

'You took an awful risk,' whispered Cara, slipping her hand into his.

Finn shrugged. 'It was a calculated one, but I was curious, and I gambled on the fact that no one would be expecting me to turn up, or even know for certain what I looked like.' He smiled. 'Looks like it was a risk that paid off.'

'You said all those awful things about Sarah,' remembered Cara. 'When I said I wanted to go to her.'

'I didn't know you then,' Finn said simply. 'I didn't know whether I could really trust you. And Sarah had told me that if you did want to get away, she wanted to be the one to tell you who she was. But now that Luca's been arrested and you know about your uncle, it seems pointless to keep it from you any longer.'

Cara was silent, turning over in her mind several things that had puzzled her since childhood and that now seemed only too plain. 'What happened between them?' she asked at last. 'Between Sarah and my uncle . . . my father?'

They sat down on the bed and Finn lifted her hand and began stroking his fingers across the back of her knuckles with that unconscious semicircular motion that she knew so well. 'They met, as far as I know, when she was on holiday in Italy,' he said. 'They had an affair, a pretty tempestuous one, by all accounts. He promised to marry her, but somehow, something went wrong and he married someone else.'

Cara nodded. 'He told me about that once, long after my aunt died, about having to follow his sense of duty.'

'Well, it can't have been too well attuned when he knew Sarah,' said Finn drily. 'Because she had a baby. You. My guess is she was too proud to tell your uncle.' He paused and glanced at her. 'Sorry, your father,' he amended. 'My guess is he found out after it was too late, and then he arranged for his brother and sister-in-law to have you.'

'And then they died,' whispered Cara. 'And Sarah came to be my nanny.'

'Must have been a pretty tough decision,' remarked Finn. 'Seeing as your father's wife was still alive. Sarah told me she never breathed a word to anybody while she was there, and she was careful never to be alone with him.' He looked into Cara's face. 'Tension in that place must have been unbelievable at times.'

'Yes,' she said, thinking of the tension she had experienced in the last few days. 'I don't know that I could stand it, myself.'

He shrugged. 'I guess, knowing Sarah, she just had to be with you, whatever the cost, while you were growing up. It would have been different if your adoptive parents hadn't died, but when you were effectively orphaned, there was no way she was going to back off.'

'But when my aunt died,' remembered Cara, 'Sarah and my uncle had that huge row, and she left.' She glanced at Finn. 'I remember that, you know. I was in the next room, and he was furious because she was refusing to marry him. He said she was breaking his heart, that she was throwing everything in his face and that she had a duty to marry him. I thought it was a lovely idea. I couldn't understand why she just went up in flames.' She paused for a moment, remembering. 'I was in an alcove, and they didn't even know I was there, and I never said anything afterwards, but I'd never, ever seen them so angry.'

'Pride,' said Finn simply.

Cara nodded. 'Yes,' she replied. 'I can see that now. He'd just expect her to marry him, and she'd think that if she wasn't good enough in the first place, she wasn't going to accept second prize.'

There was a small silence, and she shrugged helplessly. 'With parents like that I'm surprised I'm not completely unreasonable.'

Finn smiled at her, and she reddened. 'Well, I'm not,' she protested earnestly. 'Not all the time, anyway.'

'Are you going to ring her?' he asked.

Cara shook her head. 'No,' she said softly, putting her hand over her heart. 'There are too many feelings in here for just a phone call. I understand her now, when she said you weren't to tell me. I'm glad you phoned to tell her I was safe, but I want to speak to her in person. We're going to need a lot of time to sort it all out.'

Silence fell between them, each busy with thoughts. And then Cara looked up to find Finn gazing at her. There was something in his expression that made her heart start to beat very fast. 'What?' she faltered. 'What's wrong?'

'Nothing,' he replied. 'Except I was just thinking that when we get married, you are not going to run out of the church halfway through the service with some gate-crasher who thinks he knows best.'

She stared at him, her eyes wide. 'Why not?' she demanded innocently. 'I did last time, and look where it got me.'

'Come here,' he said huskily, reaching for her with a sudden hunger that she could no longer deny, and did not want to.

'Did I ever tell you how beautiful you are?' he murmured, his fingers slipping under the thin silky cotton of her dress, setting her skin on fire.

'Yes,' she whispered dreamily. 'I believe you did.'

A full moon was climbing the sky outside their window, and its silver light invaded the room, brushing everything with a cool radiance. Finn's face was half in shadow, his eyes dark and deep.

Nothing else seemed real at all, she thought vaguely, not the room or the bed, or the heady scent of lavender on the warm night air. And as he touched her, reality slipped further and further away until only they two existed.

Only the way Finn looked at her, held her, caressed her was of any importance, had any meaning in this world.

Soundlessly she gave herself up to him, her fingers, tentatively at first, exploring the smooth feel of his skin under his crisp shirt, and then, as they lay on the bed, trailing over his arms, his chest, delighting in the realisation of the pleasure she was giving him.

'I love you, Cara,' he whispered as she lay in his arms, their clothes in crazy heaps around them. So wrapped up in Finn, she was not very certain how they had got there. Mutely she gazed into his eyes and smiled. 'I know,' she murmured. 'I think I've always known.'

She had never seen such rain. It hurled itself against the windows of Sarah's elegant sitting room like bucketfuls of grapeshot, and the slate grey clouds hanging sullenly overhead looked so low Cara felt she could almost touch them.

'England in August,' drawled Sarah, lying back against her sofa cushions and drawing her feet up against her. 'Typical bank holiday weather.'

Cara turned from gazing at the water-sleek London pavements and paced towards the sofa. Her mother had to be the most elegant woman she'd ever seen. Even in jeans and an old cotton shirt, her hair—her long, thick golden hair—pulled carelessly into a knot on the back of her neck, she looked like she just stepped out of a picture in an expensive magazine.

'Darling, what is the matter?' Sarah had the same quality of amusement in her eyes that Finn had, Cara thought. Perhaps that's what had drawn her to him in the first place.

She shook her head, unwilling to give away her secret. She had promised Finn she wouldn't tell.

'Nothing,' she said as lightly as she could. 'Nothing at all.'

'Rubbish,' replied Sarah easily. 'We might have spent all those years apart, but you're still my daughter. And I know when you're lying to me.'

It was true. It had been three weeks since Finn had taken her to Sarah's spacious flat, but it was as though she had been there forever.

'I might be,' Cara agreed diffidently. 'But I promised not to tell.'

Sarah gave her one sharp glance and then looked smilingly at the ceiling. 'Finn,' she said. 'He and you are cooking something up.'

'It's just wedding plans,' Cara said earnestly.

Sarah held out a hand to her. 'He's a good man. And he's very lucky to have you.'

Cara drew a deep breath. 'I know about my father,' she said, gazing into her mother's eyes. 'Don't you think it's time we talked about it?' She thought of all the things they had talked about over the last few days, and none of them had to do with her parentage. Sarah had skirted round it, and Cara had not liked to push the subject. But now...now she had to.

Sarah sighed. 'There's not much to talk about,' she said at last. 'We fell in love and then duty dictated he marry someone else. When she died, he just thought he could pick up where he left off.' She looked straight at Cara. 'He never once apologised, you know.' There was silence and then she added, 'One word. One look and I would have been his for all time.' She shook her head. 'Such pride. Such stupid pride.'

'On both sides,' said Cara firmly.

And Sarah, after one astonished glance, laughed out loud. 'You are your father's daughter, all right,' she said at last. 'But what's to be done? There's no use crying over spilt milk.'

Cara got up once more and paced to the window. Where was Finn? He had been due ages ago. Then, as if on cue, a car swished through the puddles outside and pulled up against the pavement. She could see Finn get out of the driving seat and hurry round to the passenger door, opening an umbrella as he went. Cara pressed her nose flat against the glass to catch a glimpse of the passenger and swore as the glass misted up.

'What's so interesting?' demanded Sarah, swinging her legs off the sofa.

'Nothing,' lied Cara, edging towards the hallway, then making a bolt for the front door.

'Cara!' shouted Sarah. 'What—'

But Cara didn't hear the rest. She was too busy yanking open the door and concentrating on the men on the threshold.

The man who had been all of Cara's life was standing in front of Finn. The man she had always thought of as her uncle. He looked at her long and hard, and she smiled uncertainly at him. His attack had left him thinner than she remembered, and there was a look in his eye that she had never seen before. Humility. He touched her cheek. 'Forgive me?' he asked.

Cara gazed at him. 'There's nothing to forgive,' she said.

'I think there is,' he replied. 'I nearly ruined your life through my stupid pride.' He shook his head. 'I was too busy wanting to hurt your mother as much as I possibly could to think about your feelings.' He shrugged, raindrops glistening on his tweed coat. 'I guess I wondered if she'd try to stop the wedding. If she'd come to the church.

'I plan to make amends,' he said. 'Truly. I think every night of what I nearly forced you into and—'

Cara touched his arm. 'It's all right,' she murmured. 'Everything turned out for the best.'

He turned and smiled at Finn. 'Take her away, Cormac, and make sure you make her happy, before I change my mind about you and about helping the police.'

'Helping the police?' All three turned at Sarah's voice. She was standing in the sitting room doorway, gazing at her former lover as if they were the only two people in the world.

He stepped towards her. 'It's true,' he said softly. 'But right at this moment, none of it matters. I have lived long and done foolish things, but none was so foolish as to let you go.' He paused and then lifted his chin. 'I'm sorry, Sarah. And I want you to forgive me. Will you?'

Finn put out a hand to Cara and gently tugged her away. 'Come on,' he muttered. 'Let's leave them to it. You can catch up on all the news later. They've been waiting a long time for this moment.'

Cara glanced at her mother, the look on Sarah's face one she had never seen before.

'Sarah,' repeated the man she now knew to be her father. 'Say something, throw something at me if you want, but don't just stand there. Do you know how much I've always loved you?'

Cara looked from one to the other and then, slipping her hand into Finn's, pulled him over the threshold and closed the door behind them.

'I told you it would be a good surprise,' she said happily, gazing at him. Raindrops were trickling down his face, beading his eyelashes as he smiled at her.

'Do you think they'll throw a lot of china at each other before they make up?' he asked, as a faint crashing sound came through the door.

'Bound to,' agreed Cara. 'But one thing's for certain. Looks like we'll have more than one wedding to plan,' she said, running happily in the rain to his car.

MILLS & BOON®

Next Month's Romances

Each month you can choose from a wide variety of romance novels from Mills & Boon. Below are the new titles to look out for next month from the Presents and Enchanted series.

Presents™

SEDUCING THE ENEMY	Emma Darcy
WILDEST DREAMS	Carole Mortimer
A TYPICAL MALE!	Sally Wentworth
SETTLING THE SCORE	Sharon Kendrick
ACCIDENTAL MISTRESS	Cathy Williams
A HUSBAND FOR THE TAKING	Amanda Browning
BOOTS IN THE BEDROOM!	Alison Kelly
A MARRIAGE IN THE MAKING	Natalie Fox

Enchanted™

THE NINETY-DAY WIFE	Emma Goldrick
COURTING TROUBLE	Patricia Wilson
TWO-PARENT FAMILY	Patricia Knoll
BRIDE FOR HIRE	Jessica Hart
REBEL WITHOUT A BRIDE	Catherine Leigh
RACHEL'S CHILD	Jennifer Taylor
TEMPORARY TEXAN	Heather Allison
THIS MAN AND THIS WOMAN	Lucy Gordon

SUMMER SEARCH

How would you like to win a year's supply of Mills & Boon® books? Well you can and they're FREE! Simply complete the competition below and send it to us by 31st December 1997. The first five correct entries picked after the closing date will each win a year's subscription to the Mills & Boon series of their choice. What could be easier?

SPADE
SUNSHINE
PICNIC
BEACHBALL
SWIMMING
SUNBATHING
CLOUDLESS
FUN
TOWEL
SAND
HOLIDAY

W	Q	T	U	H	S	P	A	D	E	M	B
E	Q	R	U	O	T	T	K	I	U	I	E
N	B	G	H	L	H	G	O	D	W	K	A
I	I	O	A	I	N	E	S	W	Q	L	C
H	N	U	N	D	D	F	W	P	E	O	H
S	U	N	B	A	T	H	I	N	G	L	B
N	S	E	A	Y	F	C	M	D	A	R	A
U	B	P	K	A	N	D	M	N	U	T	L
S	E	N	L	I	Y	B	I	A	N	U	L
H	B	U	C	K	E	T	N	S	N	U	E
T	A	E	W	T	O	H	G	H	O	T	F
C	L	O	U	D	L	E	S	S	P	W	N

C7F

Please turn over for details of how to enter ☞

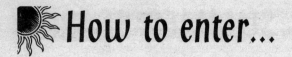 # How to enter...

Hidden in the grid are eleven different summer related words. You'll find the list beside the word puzzle overleaf and they can be read backwards, forwards, up, down and diagonally. As you find each word, circle it or put a line through it. When you have found all eleven, don't forget to fill in your name and address in the space provided below and pop this page in an envelope (you don't even need a stamp) and post it today. Hurry competition ends 31st December 1997.

Mills & Boon Summer Search Competition
FREEPOST, Croydon, Surrey, CR9 3WZ
EIRE readers send competition to PO Box 4546, Dublin 24.

Please tick the series you would like to receive if you are a winner
Presents™ ☐ Enchanted™ ☐ Temptation® ☐
Medical Romance™ ☐ Historical Romance™ ☐

Are you a Reader Service™ Subscriber?   Yes ☐   No ☐

Ms/Mrs/Miss/Mr _____
                                              (BLOCK CAPS PLEASE)

Address _____

_____

_____ Postcode _____

(I am over 18 years of age)